Searching for the
CASTLE

Searching for the

CASTLE

Backtrail of an Adoption

Barbara Leigh Ohrstrom

iUniverse LLC
Bloomington

SEARCHING FOR THE CASTLE
BACKTRAIL OF AN ADOPTION

iUniverse books may be ordered through booksellers or by contacting:

iUniverse
1663 Liberty Drive
Bloomington, IN 47403
www.iuniverse.com
1-800-Authors (1-800-288-4677)

ISBN: 978-1-4917-1306-8 (sc)
ISBN: 978-1-4917-1307-5 (hc)
ISBN: 978-1-4917-1308-2 (e)

Library of Congress Control Number: 2013919346

Printed in the United States of America.

iUniverse rev. date: 12/9/2013

The wind was crying,
not from shame.
The wind was crying,
for it knew not its name.

Dedicated to

Gladys Strong, who gave me my only childhood home.

Kristin Gustafson, who believed in me.

Nancy Holt, who knows who I am.

Contents

Preface

I WANT TO THANK EACH and every one of you who reads this book. This is not a story with a happy ending, or even a wonderful beginning. It is not easy to read about another's life when injustice and harm have caused suffering. Oftentimes, these types of stories stir feelings of rage, helplessness, and grief in the reader—and that may very well mean you. So I thank you.

By many definitions, I am a successful woman. I love what I do—I teach writing. I teach people to express their identity, to write and discover who they are, from where they come, what is strong about them, where they have shown courage, when they have given kindnesses. Through this, I hope to teach people their suffering has meaning even if that meaning proves elusive.

How prophetic are those words! While I have taught students since 1987, the meaning of my story has eluded me.

I discovered the meaning of my story through the eyes of two other people. First, as we walked through Arnold Arboretum in Jamaica Plain, a former boss and friend told me she had never seen any teacher give tough love in such an effective way. She said, "Students hear you because there is no ego attached." That has to be one of the kindest and most flattering statements anyone has said to me.

Later that week, on a night when a colleague and friend and I were tired, we still met for drinks and dinner. I had been struggling with the social mechanics of work. "I feel like an outsider in my department," I told her. She knows a bit of my story—enough so in a rare moment of vulnerability, I told her a part of me always feels sad. A part of me always struggles to belong. A part of me always feels I must always not only do, but also be my best, so I will be allowed to stay, to belong, to be loved. She nodded, and then the discussion, as it frequently does when teachers sit together, moved on to students.

We teach students who feel alienated from society—they are "urban youth," the euphemism for black and brown kids who have grown up undereducated. Many of them also have grown up in the maelstrom of violence that poverty brings. Many have suffered losses: parents, siblings, cousins, friends—some to illnesses and some to violence. Nearly all of our students are trauma survivors. So we had, as you might imagine, a lot to discuss.

But toward the end of that evening, my colleague looked at me. "Your wound is also a shining, multifaceted gem," she said. "You can connect to the students in ways others cannot." That is true. This ability to connect feels like a gift.

I felt this gift the first time when I was fifteen. I sat in the pouring rain with another kid, who was determined to run away from home. But through an hour of discussion, I convinced her the world would devour her, and she must go home. Finally, she turned back, back toward home. I too went home, with rainwater dripping off my hair, in my eyes, off every inch of my clothing.

That is the first time I shared knowledge in such a way so that someone could integrate this new knowledge and act on her own behalf. Two years later, I ran away to a therapeutic community, Odyssey House, for teenagers and adults. Then I began tutoring other kids at Odyssey House—kids with third-grade reading levels, kids who couldn't spell, kids who felt ashamed because of their lack of skills. I knew what those kids felt: shame, loneliness, fear, vulnerability; they constantly issued silent cries for real help to shoulder such burdens. Those kids needed to feel their emotions were understandable. These students were intelligent; once they knew their lack of skill would be interpreted as lack of skill rather than lack of character, they felt safe enough to learn.

I have been a teacher all my life. I love teaching. Sometimes I have occasion to reread some of the notes students have given me, or the recommendation letters people have written for me, and I am still awed. I have taught in Boston, San Francisco, and Ann Arbor. I have taught the rich, the poor, the middle and upper classes. I have taught international students from nearly every country and certainly every continent on earth. I have taught teachers. In short, as one of my former deans put it, I can teach anything that moves because I am in love with writing itself. I am in love with what I do and who I am as I do it.

At the very root of this profession that has given me so much is one central truth: I am gifted at what I do because my terrible wound of alienation and not belonging gives me empathy for any kind of student. At heart, my students feel they don't belong. When they come to me, I say, "Yes, you do. No matter what your story, nationality, ability, gender, age, or class, no matter your trauma, your hurts, your wounds that won't heal, you are my student now. Mine. And you belong. We will do this together. You are not alone now; you are with me, and I will help you learn, step-by-step. I will not abandon you nor leave you to struggle in the terrible silence of knowing no help is to be had."

Would I have been the teacher I am without the wound of losing my birth parents? Without losing my foster family who loved me so much? I think not. It took my colleague to show me this.

The meaning of these events you are about to read is the story of injustice and suffering. But it also is the story of redemption, courage, and the origins of that multifaceted gem my colleague showed me. This work—changing the world one moment, one student at a time—has occupied my professional life, and because of it, I have earned self-respect, reputation, and honor. Because of it, I have known happiness, and that happiness feels as real as the sadness at the events of the infancy, toddler, child, and adolescent stages of my life.

I thank the Creator this is so. My life has been filled with meaning and significance beyond what I had dreamed, and I am, and always will be, grateful to my Creator for giving me this day, these students, this life.

Foreword

(Essay written by Barbara Gay Power, my foster sister.)

PEARLY WHITE AND PINK, ALMOST fluorescent, softly wrinkled, fragile-looking, yet hard to the touch—on the inside of an oyster shell, its beauty would be exquisite. On the back of a two-year old female child, it was horrifying and fascinating. Her social worker explained to us she had been scalded by a hot water tap, left running while she was unattended. This grapefruit-sized scar was surrounded from armpits to knees by small, pus-filled sores. "She shows signs of neglect, and we know she has been confined to a crib for months. We fear there may be retardation, and of course, if that is the case, she will be institutionalized."

My mother, thin-lipped at this recital, scooped up the sad scrap of a baby and cradled her, while responding, "Well, let's just see how she does."

This was our introduction to Billy, Barbara, and Susan. I was thirteen when my parents decided to take in foster children. These were our first arrivals, and everyone was excited and apprehensive. They came two days before Christmas 1962, after my mother (with two days notice) had frantically pulled together clothing, cribs, bedding, snowsuits, toys, and Christmas presents.

Susan was three, frightened, skinny, nervous, and wary. A pretty little slip of a child, she seemed so eager to please, her eyes darting from one giant human to another, looking for someplace to connect. Her little hands picked at one another and kept straying to a sore on the corner of her mouth. My father settled her on his lap, where she, with the attention span of any three-year-old, became captivated by the reflection of the Christmas lights on his glasses.

Her brother and sister, Billy and Barbie, were two-year-old twins. Barbie, neglected, forgotten, and abused, was limp in my mother's arms. My brother, Dana, age eleven, sat nearby and regarded her with curiosity. She didn't coo, wiggle, or respond. Dana's eyes darted back and forth between her face and my mother's, fearing the social worker's words were true. Billy, her polar opposite, made his way around the room, hanging onto furniture, legs, hands. He chattered and laughed and touched everyone. My older sister, Patti, was enthralled by his beauty: big brown eyes, rosy skin, and sandy-color straight hair. He soon had a Christmas ball in each hand and was tottering after our aged family dog while the dog looked over her shoulder in distress.

The social worker, after explaining medical forms, clothing allowances, and other budgetary constraints left—just left. Our family instantaneously grew from five to eight; we now had a potentially institution-bound child and her siblings on our hands, and it was Christmas.

I don't know how my parents did it, but the new family just evolved. I don't remember any traumatic adjustments; no one was lost in the shuffle. The house seemed to grow to accommodate us all; meals were plain and noisy; there were mountains of laundry; toys and books abounded; everyone flourished. We squabbled, made up, laughed, cried, called each other names, picked on each other, and became a unit.

Over the years, Susan lost her nervous fawn-ready-to-flee posture. She flitted from one room to the next, always twirling the dresses she insisted on wearing. My sister and she spent hours playing dress-up and hairdresser and dancers. Her feet never seemed to touch the ground. On her first day of kindergarten, she turned on the school bus steps, blew a wet, smacking kiss, and went off to conquer the world. No fear here.

Billy was everyone's boy. I can see him sledding in the pasture behind my parents' house, the wind and excitement whipping his cheeks red. He never lost his fascination for the dog, and she, old as she was, made Billy her charge. If Billy were in the yard swinging, his canine buddy was nearby. If Billy were watching TV, the old mutt was his pillow. As he grew older, his baby beauty turned to handsomeness. He was always happy, this boy of ours, and smart and eager to learn.

Barbie became my mother's special project. That coldhearted fish of a social worker had thrown down a gauntlet, and my mother, with Barbie's life hanging in the balance, snatched it up. She never stopped teaching her. Everything was explained, pronounced, spelled, touched, and described. She worked with those frail limbs, kneading, exercising, stretching, and bending. She was Barbie's coach; we were the cheerleaders, and by God, Barbie did it. Barbie walked, talked, sang, colored, danced, caught up with the other kids, even passed many. Her favorite cry, flopping on my lap, was always, "Read to me." She was a joy and a clown. She and I were inseparable, sharing even a name.

They took them away in my senior year. I came home from school to find my mother, white-faced, sitting on the couch. She was stricken as she explained to me the state had found an adoptive family for all three children. My seventeen-year-old brain couldn't grasp the news. I cried. I went numb. "Why, Mom, why?" I demanded to know.

My mother woodenly explained that she and my father had signed a contract with the state, four years prior, that they wouldn't try to adopt the children should an adoptive family be found. The odds had been miniscule that a home would be found. (No one would want to adopt three older children.) She and my father didn't have the money to engage in a legal battle. Besides, it was good. The kids would have good parents; they would be together; they would have all the advantages that my parents, with six children, could ill-afford. She said all the right things. Neither of us believed them. This was a Monday. They were to leave on Friday.

Our home was a den of contradiction. For the little ones, everything was normal. For the rest of us, anguish and disbelief reigned. Our grief was enormous and controlled. I thought of kidnapping them and running away. I composed a long letter to their adoptive parents to put in their suitcase, begging their adoptive parents to let them come home. I tore it up. I cried endlessly as my parents quietly packed and called relatives.

How do you tell your babies that they have to go away, that they will never see you again? How do you tear those little arms from your neck? How do you answer when little trusting Susan asks, "But don't you love us anymore?" I don't know how my parents coped. My heart broke.

I wish I could say that was the end. I wish the state, in its infinite wisdom, had made magic happen for my foster brother and sisters, but in its zeal to "place" these children, they consigned them to a living hell. It shouldn't have happened.

We were to never know where they were. Perhaps that hurt the most, not knowing, but my aunt Grace, one day while reading the *Boston Globe*, came across a thank you letter from an adoptive parent. This woman was thanking an unknown foster mother for raising her very special children, twins and their sister. She signed herself "Mizpah," a Christian blessing. My dear Aunt Grace wrote to the woman through the *Globe*; the letter was forwarded, addresses were exchanged, and by some miracle, my mother was corresponding with the adoptive mother. The kids were okay. Medical histories were filled in, anecdotes recounted, and we told ourselves that they were all right. Marie, their new adoptive mom, said so. She sent pictures. To me, they looked sad, but that may been my still-grieving teenage imagination. She assured us they were fine.

As they got older, the pictures showed tall, coltish, gawky adolescents. I was sure they still looked sad and hollow-eyed, and amazingly, they resembled their adoptive parents. All were unsmiling and what my father called "camera-shy." One wouldn't call them an attractive family. The letters became fewer as everyone's lives got busier and went in different directions. My brother, sister, and I married and had children of our own. Billy, Barbie, and Susan were off to college, Marie said, and life went on …

Still, a system that absolves itself through a litany of facts, figures, stats, and procedures tore them from us and dared them to survive. Numbers were analyzed and tallied to justify voracious budgetary requirements, and three little souls were no longer on the state's roles. Mission accomplished.

My parents' rage is justified. I can only ache for Billy, Barbara, and Susan and their lost childhoods and tormented adulthoods. I think of them often. We loved these children; we were a family.

CHAPTER 1

Beginning the Search

December 1978
24 West Twelfth Street
Odyssey House
New York, NY

It was dark and late, and I was awake. I stared at the light from the streetlamp coming through the window and glimmering across the wooden, polished floor of the therapeutic community where I lived. An hour passed and then another hour. I rose and walked through the large building in the dark to my drafting desk, where I worked during the day delivering packages, creating graphics, and running the old Gestetner printing press. I turned on a single overhead light and placed a sheet of white paper in front of me.

If only, I thought, my memory would focus. The blank piece of paper became a fuzzy projection screen, like the kind in my earth science class in my high school, from which I had graduated eighteen months earlier.

I remembered getting adopted when I was five. My first time riding a subway left me dizzy and elated as I had spun myself around on the silver poles in the middle of the car. We entered a majestic building in Boston, and I cut my knee when I had fallen on an escalator. The judge had seemed otherworldly as he sat atop a dais, encased in a wooden

1

stand so only his black-robed chest and shoulders showed. He called me all the way up to his dais and asked me to spell my middle name for him. In the car, on the way back to New Hampshire, I asked Marie, my new adoptive mother, what being adopted meant. "It means I am your mother," she said.

And then, confused, I asked, "Does everyone have more than one mommy?" She hadn't answered me, but Al, my new father, said none of us—me, my sister, or my twin brother—should say the word *adoption* ever again.

I remembered Sue talked about our rocking chairs from when we were little kids, but I didn't remember the chairs. My adoptive parents said they didn't know anything about rocking chairs. Once, I found Sue wandering in the basement, and I asked what she was doing. Hopeless, she had answered, "Looking for our rocking chairs."

I remembered Sue also owned a book she liked a lot. Here my memory wobbled, and I closed my eyes in an effort to see: a horse on the cover. I tried to see what Sue was doing with the book, and the memory, sharp and sudden, came. Reading the book, she and I had sat on the bed. Al had appeared, wanting to know where we got the book. Sue handed it to him, and he glanced at the inside cover, clenched his jaw, and took the book away.

I snapped open my eyes—the inside cover. I closed my eyes again, straining to make the image of the inside cover appear, but could see nothing except letters that would not completely form. I could not remember most of my life up to age five; I had thought that was normal until some Odyssey House kids told me they remembered events from when they were two. I lit a cigarette. Those letters might be important, and my twin brother, Bill, might know what they were. I could sleep now and returned upstairs to my bedroom.

The next morning, I went to Sixth Street Odyssey House and found my twin, Bill. "Bill, I have to talk to you." I shepherded him inside an empty conference room, shut the door, and locked it. "Listen," I said. "Last night, I remembered that book, the one Sue had when we got taken away from the Powers. It had a picture of a horse on the front, remember?"

"Yeah, it was *Mr. Ed, the Talking Horse.*"

"Remember Dad got mad and took the book away from her?"

Bill looked at me like I'd lost my mind.

"Dad took it away for a reason, right? He looked at the inside cover, saw something in there, and it made him mad." I paused. "I think it was a name."

"So what was so special about a name?"

"Bill, what was the name? Do you remember the name?"

"Yeah, course I do. Orstom, or something like that."

"That's it, Bill, that's it."

"What's it?"

"That's our name!"

"No, that's our foster mother's name."

"No, Bill, listen. Mom wrote that sentimental letter to Confidential Chat (similar to Dear Abby), right? And our foster mother figured out she was writing about us and wrote to Confidential Chat and had Confidential Chat contact Mom. Our foster parents' last name was Power, not Orstom or whatever it is."

"My God," he said.

"That's what I'm telling you, Bill. You remembered our real last name."

"My God," he repeated.

I left him and tramped back to Twelfth Street Odyssey House, where I lived. Who had written the name inside the book? Could it be my mother's actual handwriting? Did the book still exist?

The next day, I wrote a letter to my adoptive mother and pleaded with her to break into my adoptive father's filing cabinet and get the adoption records. I told her that although I knew my adoptive father wouldn't want her to help me, I had to have this information. As I licked the envelope, I prayed she would understand why I needed the information; I prayed she would help me.

Meanwhile, Bill persuaded a Massachusetts phone operator to look through every listing in Massachusetts and got the address and telephone number of the Powers, our foster parents. I was too afraid to call the

Powers after all these years, so I wrote another letter, this time to my foster mother.

I waited. December slid into January. I incessantly bugged Jack, the guy who manned the front reception desk of Odyssey House. "Is the mail here yet? Any mail for me today?"

"Relax!" he growled. "I'll tell ya, ya got any mail!" One day he handed me a slim manila envelope. "Hope that's what you want," he said.

I didn't answer him. The package was from my adoptive mother. I ripped it open with shaking hands.

The first page was a letter from Ms. Frost, a social worker I remembered who had worn Coke-bottle glasses. The letter congratulated Al and Marie and confirmed the court date for the adoption. I scanned it impatiently and put it down. The second page was a letter from the Department of Welfare, stating that Al and Marie's home had been accepted "for the placement of an adopted child or children." The third page, a form, stated that according to the Division of Child Guardianship, I had, indeed, been born. Ms. Frost signed it on July 29, 1965, eight days before my fifth birthday.

The fourth page, another letter from Ms. Frost dated July 9, 1965, was rather chatty, discussing our vaccinations, the status of our education (none), and pictures taken of us with Santa Claus when we lived with our foster parents. She said we were of "Portuguese and English ancestry."

I slowly turned over the last page and stared. It was the first time I had seen my fake birth certificate. It named me Barbara Malfide, born August 6, 1960. It called Marie my birth mother and Al my birth father. It claimed I was Portuguese and English. Aside from my date of birth, it stated one true fact: I am a twin.

Dated July 22, 1966, nearly six years after I was born, the oath on the bottom read: "I, Tony Bachieri, depose and say that I hold the office of Town Clerk of the Town of Wareham, County Plymouth and Commonwealth of Massachusetts; that the records of Births, Marriages and Deaths required by law to be kept in said Town are in my custody, and the above is a true extract from the records of Births in said Town, as certified by me."

Commonwealth of Massachusetts

United States of America

CERTIFICATE OF BIRTH

From the Records of Births in the Town of

WAREHAM, MASSACHUSETTS, U. S. A.

1.	Date of Birth	August 6, 1960		
2.	Full Name of Child	Barbara Leigh ▇▇▇		
3.	Sex, Color, and if Twin	Female - Twin 1		
4.	Place of Birth	Wareham, Mass.	Color	white
5.	Residence of Parents	Salisbury, New Hampshire		
6.	Name of Father	Elwood Wilbur ▇▇▇		
7.	Occupation of Father	Store Manager		
8.	Birthplace of Father	Lynn, Mass.		
9.	Maiden Name of Mother	Marie Dorothy ▇▇▇		
10.	Birthplace of Mother	Peabody, Mass.		
11.	Date of Record	August 15, 1960		

I, TONY BACCHIERI

depose and say that I hold the office of Town Clerk of the Town of Wareham, County of Plymouth and Commonwealth of Massachusetts; that the records of Births, Marriages and Deaths required by law be kept in said Town are in my custody, and that the above is a true extract from the records of Births in said Town, as certified by me.

Witness my hand and the seal of said Town,

on the .... 22nd .... day of .... July 19 66

Tony Bacchieri

TOWN CLERK.

Where were my parents' names? Where were my footprints and thumbprints? Where were my weight, height, and time of birth? Where was my name? According to this birth certificate, I came from Marie's womb nearly six years before I actually met her. Where was my real birth certificate?

I threw the papers down and exploded out the door. I ran down Twelfth Street, turned onto Sixth Avenue, and ran up Fourteenth Street, past the hookers and hustlers, the watch sellers and office workers. I jumped over fire hydrants and pushed people aside, leaving behind a trail of shocked and angry pedestrians. I ran through Union Park, up Fifteenth Street, and veered toward Eighteenth Street. I ran until I thought my lungs would burst; I ran until I felt like vomiting. I stopped and collapsed on a bench next to a dealer, bracing myself with my hands gripping my thighs, gasping for air.

Even the drug dealer had a family history, ancestors. It seemed everyone had curios from Europe, sepia photographs of ancestors, fathers, and/or mothers they looked like, and stories of when they were babies. Daughters had taken after great aunts on the mother's side of the family, or sons acted like grandfathers on the father's side of the family. Someone's chin looked exactly like the chin of a long-dead ancestor in a stained and battered photo. Even Christianity and Judaism told us all we came from Adam and Eve.

I wanted to know who I came from and why my mother gave me, Bill, and Sue away. As a child, I had daydreamed my mother and father had crashed their car or died in a falling airplane. I had dreamed my mother took us to gardens, museums, and symphonies and fantasized my father beat Al because Al had hurt me so badly. I had thought of them every single day. What tore apart our family? Why had Al locked in his steel file cabinet these worthless, lying papers? Why did the Commonwealth of Massachusetts lie?

It made no sense to me. I had no idea what the commonwealth had buried, but I knew I'd find out. Let the state lie. Let Al, Marie—let everybody—lie. I would find what I was looking for if I had to rip the country apart, brick by brick. I looked at the dealer.

He said, "Tough day, huh, kid?"

I smiled a little. "Yeah." I got up and walked home.

After looking at the papers again, an idea gripped me. The papers said I was born in Wareham, Massachusetts. Since I was born in 1960 but not adopted until 1966, the hospital records might still be on file. Maybe the commonwealth, in its zeal to "protect me" from my past, had locked the windows and doors, but left the cellar open. What if no one had destroyed the hospital records of my birth? I called directory assistance and found a single hospital in Wareham, Tobey Hospital. I decided to go there as soon as possible and see if the hospital had kept the birth records for a Barbara Orstom.

FEBRUARY 21, 1979
ODYSSEY HOUSE
30 WINNACUNNET ROAD
HAMPTON, NEW HAMPSHIRE

Today, the snow crunched under the tires of my friend Tom's car, and the sun glancing off the snow blinded me as we made our way to Tobey Hospital. Tom's status as a war veteran qualified him beyond any degree he had earned: he knew war, chaos, and suffering, circumstances familiar in my life. We had spent long hours talking, or rather, I had talked about the fire within me to find my birth parents, to find a family, and he had listened.

Tom had a craggily handsome face. His jaw was square, hair curly, eyes bluish gray, with a deeper shadow within them. He always smelled clean—not soapy clean, but healthy clean, like a man who spent every spare moment outdoors swimming in pristine lakes or climbing snowy mountains. Despite what he must have seen in combat, he was cheerful, optimistic, and kind. He could not tolerate the violence "bad" kids like me told him about; his eyes would fill with compassion and rage.

That's why I loved him. He had done his time in his war zone. As I thought about him, our long drive to Wareham passed slowly. Anxious thoughts gripped me, so many events could go awry. I could have the wrong name. The clerk could deny me my records. The records might not exist. Toward Wareham, I blustered, hiding my fear. "If they don't gimme the records, I'm gonna take 'em anyway. I'll go right over the counter and punch the clerk in the head. I'll go through all those file cabinets 'til I find 'em."

Tom said nothing.

I lapsed back into silence.

"Tom, I won't break any laws," I said after a lengthy pause.

"I know."

"They just wouldn't have the records and then not give them to me, would they?"

"I don't know. Maybe."

When we pulled into Wareham, I said, "Wait. Let's go to the beach."

He pulled into the parking lot abutting the tiny town beach. I got out and walked by the water. I had stood on this same beach three days before I ran away to Odyssey House because I wanted to see the town in which I was born. Now I wanted the ocean to calm me and stop my hands from shaking when I walked into the hospital and asked for my records.

I climbed into the car. "Okay, let's do it."

Although Tobey Hospital was built on top of a hill, it was still unimposing; it reminded me of my grammar school. Few cars were parked on the gray pavement with the faded lines. No one, I hoped, was going to be rigid or rule-conscious here.

I got out of the car and walked through the clean glass doors. The information clerk directed me to the records department around the corner. *Good,* I thought, *an easy exit.* Tom walked behind me, and we entered the records department. Looking bored, a young man stood behind the counter. I told him I wanted my birth records.

"Spell your last name, please."

"O-r-s-t-o-m."

"Just a moment." He disappeared.

The slowest ten minutes of my life drifted by, marked by the huge Seth Thomas clock on the yellow wall. *My sister Sue worked at a Seth Thomas factory,* I thought idly, and the young man returned.

I felt certain he had not found the records. Worse, he had them

8

and would not give them to me. But he had papers in his hand, and he walked past me and sat at a desk in the room. I followed him and reached for the records, willing my left hand not to shake. He pulled the papers away from me.

"I need you to sign this release and consent form," he said.

I'll sign anything, I thought. *Just give me the records.* I signed quickly and pushed the paper at him. He glanced at the signature. "I need your maiden name," he said.

I did not know my name. I tried to see the papers in his hand and read my name upside down, but I could only see enough to know my version of my name had two missing letters, so I signed Barbara Orstom and placed the pen exactly over my signature. I again reached out. He again held the papers back.

"That'll be $1.40 for the copying fees," he said.

I fumbled in my pocket for the money and heard Tom's steady, reassuring voice behind me.

"Here it is." Tom stretched over my shoulder and handed the man the money.

I reached for my records a third time, and the man handed them to me.

I mumbled, "Thank you," and forced my legs to walk, not run. I waited for the arresting hand to clamp onto my shoulder, spin me around, and take the records away from me. It never came. Tom and I pushed through those clean, glass doors. I had my identity in my hands.

I ran through the parking lot and leaped in the air, joy bursting through every cell in my body. It was the happiest moment of my life.

Tom grinned laconically and sauntered over to the car.

"Come on, Tom, let's get the hell out of here!"

When we sat in the car with the doors locked, I looked at the three pages printed from microfiche.

The first fact I saw was the spelling of my name—O-h-r-s-t-r-o-m, not Orstom. My full name is Barbara Leigh Ohrstrom. I weighed five pounds and eleven ounces" at birth and measured eighteen inches long. I was born at 1:04 p.m. on August 6, 1960. (No wonder I hated getting up in the morning!)

My mother's name is Joan A. Ohrstrom; her given name was Morris, and she was thirty-three years old that day in 1960. She was employed as a housewife. My father's name is William F. Ohrstrom, and he was thirty years old in 1960. They were married. That was a surprise; I had been given the impression adoptees' mothers, poor teenagers, never married. My father worked as a bartender. They lived on Williams Avenue, Wareham, Massachusetts. The next page listed medical stuff I didn't understand about shots and eyedrops of silver nitrate. A Dr. Nye had delivered Bill and me. The next page repeated a lot of information and added some more details. My father had been born in Worcester, Massachusetts, and my mother in Boston, and he had been employed at the Surrey Room in Wareham, Massachusetts.

I looked out the car window. Tom had parked at the little beach again to let me read everything. "Tom, let's go over to this Williams Avenue and check out the house."

We found it easily enough, and Tom stopped across the street. I got out of the car and figured the owner was away because no cars sat in the driveway. I peered in the windows and felt like a thief stealing glimpses into someone else's life to try to find a piece of my own. Sun lit the house, and the hardwood floors gleamed with polish. I imagined I crawled across those floors sixteen years earlier.

We returned to Hampton. When we got to Hampton, I didn't talk much about what I'd found; it felt too precious. I wanted to first treasure it alone. On the train back to New York the next day, I wrote my name in a sketch pad—big letters, small, red ink, blue, green, horizontal, vertical. I felt the ecstasy lovers feel, the impulse to laugh and smile to myself. Instead of shouting my new lover's name to the world, I wanted to shout my own.

The train pulled into Penn Station. I felt tired, yet my mind wouldn't stop churning. My far-fetched notion had worked. Now all I had to do was find my parents. Maybe I should move back to New Hampshire; places I might need to go would be closer.

I couldn't wait to tell Bill all that had happened at the hospital, so I stopped at Sixth Street Odyssey House to tell him. (At that time, Odyssey House, a therapeutic treatment program for adults and adolescents, had facilities in four states, including four in New York City.) Bill was flabbergasted, then elated. He hadn't believed I could pull it off, but now he didn't think finding our parents would be hard. He told me he would start calling directory assistance and bugging them again.

When I arrived home at Twelfth Street, a letter from my foster mother, Gladys Power, waited for me.

JANUARY 18, 1979

Dear Barbara,

I was so happy that you took the time to write to me. After all these years we certainly will have a lot to write, so much that I'm not sure where to begin.

Naturally, I'm sad that you have had a bad time and were on drugs. I neither condemn nor condone your use of them. I'm sure you've heard all the preaching you care to. I'm happy to hear you are doing so well and am sure you will be fine. It's good that you and Billy are together. I hope you are as close as Pat, Barb, and Dana are.

Perhaps you should know that I did not know you were unaware that your adoptive mother was writing me and sending me pictures. I assumed (wrongly) that she had told you about our family and that you had lived in West Boylston for quite some time before being adopted. She was very proud of all of you and your accomplishments. If you do not mind, I am going to write to her and tell her that we are going to correspond.

JANUARY 22

I had started this at work, and it's two days later and I'm home. I work in the records department of a health center in Worcester. It's in the low-cost housing development for mostly Spanish and black people. I'm taking a course to be registered by the state so I can run the department by myself—with help, of course.

I'm sure you have a million questions, as have I. Maybe I can tell you a little about the time you spent here. You came in December 1962 just before Christmas only to stay for a while, but as it happened, you stayed until you were adopted. We didn't have much money, but we managed. You were very tiny and didn't walk or talk, Billy was a handsome little devil, and Susan was very shy and tried so hard to be good all the time. As time went on, the state assured us you would be with us until you were adults, but it just wasn't meant to be. A social worker called on Monday, and you were with your new parents by Friday. But the years you were with us were happy ones for us, though at times very trying— six children is not easy. I worked weekends as a waitress at the country club, and my husband Bill and the girls had to babysit all of you.

Some day when we meet, we can sit down and talk for hours about all of this. Tell me about going to college. Where is St. John's University? How are you financing it, etc.? I want to hear all about it.

Please ask Billy and Susan to write. Next time I'll write more about the kids and their kids. We have four grandchildren, but I have to go to work now. We had a terrible ice storm yesterday, so I have to allow a little more time. I have an old beat-up '67 Mustang that only goes when it wants to.

Please keep up the good work. Give my best to Billy and Susan. Write soon.

Love,

Gladys

When I showed Bill this letter, he said, "No wonder you're so determined. You had to fight for your life at such a young age." My friends were elated at the news of the name discovery and of Gladys's letter. I brightened. As my parents were married, I could find them more easily. They had not surrendered us to the commonwealth at birth; maybe they didn't want to give us away. Maybe my parents loved me. And if my parents loved me, maybe they would not be too angry when I found them.

ADOPTEES' LIBERTY MOVEMENT ASSOCIATION
PO BOX 154 WASHINGTON BRIDGE STATION · NEW YORK NY 10033

FLORENCE FISHER, PRESIDENT
(212) 581-1568

Hello and Welcome to ALMA!

Enclosed is your copy of the "Reg Niles Searchbook - Special ALMA Edition" and your ALMA membership card which assures that you were registered into the ALMA International Reunion Registry Databank immediately upon receipt of your registration fee.

In addition to your entry into the ALMA Databank, your registration fee entitles you to free membership in ALMA for the remainder of the calendar year ending December 31, 1979. PLEASE REMEMBER IT IS TAX-DEDUCTIBLE.

YOU are now a member of the largest organization of adult adoptees and natural parents in the world. We welcome you and hope that you will be as proud to be a part of ALMA as we are happy to have you.

Sincerely,

Florence Anna Fisher
President

I wrote to the Adoptees' Liberation Movement Association (ALMA) the next day and applied for membership. I had read Florence Fischer's book *The Search for Florence Fischer* as a teenager but had not realized she had founded this organization. It made me feel less alone and afraid that I was somehow wrong to want to search; other adoptees searched too.

Since I thought it would make my search easier, I decided to move to

New Hampshire in June, even though I had been admitted to St. John's University in New York. I could apply to and attend the University of New Hampshire (UNH), instead of St. John's University. My need to search consumed me so powerfully I was willing to separate from Bill, even though I had run away from home on November 2, 1977, to join him and had then moved to New York in June 1978, again to join him. I loved my twin more fiercely and deeply than anyone alive; I always had. I had nearly gone out of my mind missing him when a court had remanded him to Odyssey House in 1976.

In New York, we spent a lot of time together. We would talk about our futures and take long walks. Although Bill told me the search was more important to me than to him, he still helped. We called directory assistance in dozens of area codes, looking for Ohrstroms, as we thought Morris, our mother's maiden name, was too common. I found a Valborg Ohrstrom in Worcester, Massachusetts, but she denied knowing my father or anything about us. I sensed she did know my father, but I did not know what to say to convince her to tell me what she knew.

I wanted to tell her how much I needed to know what had happened to me, but all my life I had heard people who surrendered their kids for adoption didn't want them and didn't want to be found or bothered when their kids grew up. Newspapers printed stories about judges denying adoptees access to their records even if they had rare diseases and would die without transplants from blood relatives. Somehow these stories fascinated me, yet filled me with shame.

A tiny voice inside said if my mother and father had loved me, they wouldn't have given me away. Now it felt like Valborg wanted me to shut up and stop asking questions. I chewed my lower lip. How could I explain to Valborg how much I wanted to know my father and mother? I did not want to hurt them. I wanted them to be my parents; I wanted a family. But I just could not tell her; I could barely admit it to myself.

Two months passed, and in those two months, I worked Monday through Friday at the Odyssey House graphics department. I attended therapy groups. I squeezed in as many visits with Bill as I possibly could. Bill and I made dozens of fruitless phone calls to directory assistance.

I didn't know enough area codes or how to find more—it seemed I needed every area code in the country.

One day in late March, while idly plying the Manhattan white pages, I found a listing for a Joan A. Morris. I was elated, shaken, and ambivalent. What if it she were my mother? What would I say? What if she hung up on me? What if she lied? Then I would never know my mother.

Despite common sense telling me the chances were slim this Joan A. Morris was my mother, I desperately believed she was, and this terrified me.

I called my friend Michael. "Michael, I need a favor."

"What?"

"I found this listing for a Joan A. Morris on Christopher Street, and I'm scared to call."

"It's too late to call. Call tomorrow."

"I'm scared tomorrow."

"I'll call."

"No!"

"Look, if you can't call, I'll call. Meet me tomorrow afternoon at Sixth Street."

"Okay." I hung up the phone. That night, I watched old westerns without seeing them—and played movies of meeting my mother instead. She'd hate me; she'd slam the door in my face; she'd be elegant, and I'd be an ugly hick to her. She'd … I didn't know. In those moments, I believed I had found my mother, and as the night crawled forward, I wrote a terrible poem.

CLOSE TO HOME

Late at night, 'round three o'clock, I think of you.
Carefree days and summer nights, I imagine you.
Here it is, and I'm back in the morning again
And the following eve will bring us both much pain,
But the morrow's morn could give much to gain.

Some time ago—what happened to bring us here?
Did you cry in sorrow, or turn without a tear?
Has life closed the chasm, or was there a gap to fill?

You gave me life years ago.
Does it matter if I ever show?

No more pictures, no more scenes.
What's real is coming close, it seems.
No more thoughtful summer nights.
Far off a lullaby plays,
Peaceful in the yesterdays,
And hours away it'll be a new morn;
A different kind of child will be born.
It'll hurt, but all hurt ends.
Yes, I want to walk with you ...
talk with you.
The sun is rising.
We might be able to
go from here.

Tense and silent, I worked all day with Bobby, my boss at the graphics department, then ran to Sixth Street and burst into Michael's office on the second floor.

"Well?" I asked.

"She's not your mother."

"Her name is the same, right down to the middle initial."

"She never heard of William Ohrstrom."

"She could have lied."

"Barbara," he said, patient, talking to a stubborn child, "I had to repeat his name to her. She's not lying."

Feeling deflated and a little foolish, I collapsed into a chair. Of course this search would not be finished by simply taking a name out of the Manhattan white pages. This would not be my only defeat; I had better get used to it now. Nevertheless, somehow, someway, this search had to work out—I had the names, and that made future searching easier. Since my information indicated I needed to concentrate on Massachusetts, and since New Hampshire was much closer to Massachusetts than New York, the search, I decided, had to go into limbo until I moved to New Hampshire to go to college.

Bill agreed with me, pointing out his interest reached only to helping me, not to actually finding anyone.

Did he not burn with that fire because he did not need parents and I did? Was it because he knew no magical family would exist? Is that what I thought—a magical family existed? No, but my parents were real; I could not turn from the possibility of them being family. Maybe they had wanted us; maybe they still wanted us.

I felt disappointed he did not burn with the same fire to know. Maybe "disappointed" did not quite fit. Maybe I felt less justified, more of that shame and confusing guilt. Maybe I wanted his help because it helped justify searching. But I can't hurry the sunrise, I told myself, and I can't make my twin brother burn to search.

I didn't know why the damn search consumed me in light of it seeming unimportant not only to Bill, but also to so many other people. All my arguments sounded weak; I just didn't know what would make people understand. It felt like the craziness of being in love, except instead of thinking about my beloved all the time, I thought about searching. How can someone explain love? How could I explain my search?

Despite those doubtful thoughts, on June 1, 1979, a year after my move to New York, I again packed my few possessions and said my good-byes. Michael's girlfriend Leslie, Michael, and I stopped at Sixth Street Odyssey House so I could run in and hug Bill good-bye one last time. I jumped into the U-Haul, and Leslie pulled away, lurching through the potholes. I saw the sun set over the Triboro Bridge, and then I turned from my life in New York.

Ahead lay the dull lights of suburbs, which would eventually give way to the yellow dots of small towns. Ahead lay the highways through Massachusetts and New Hampshire—and the Welcome to New Hampshire sign. Ahead lay the whereabouts of my parents.

June 26, 1979
Hampton, New Hampshire

I woke up sweating. It felt like a day in August, when the dogs lie down and pant at nine o'clock in the morning. Damp with sweat, the sheets were tangled around my legs. I jumped out of bed quickly as soon as the fog of sleep cleared; I was going to court today.

I figured the county court would be located near the town hall, so I asked my friend Martin to drop me there. He drove off, and I bounded up the stairs. Two minutes later, I dragged myself out of the town hall with my head bowed. The county court was two miles away. I held two pieces of paper in my hand: my court appearance sheet and the birth certificate my adoptive mother had sent me. The sweat from my hands mottled the paper; sweat ran down my neck and back and stained my shirt.

As I walked, my thoughts echoed voices in yet another mind movie.

Your father could be a criminal.

Your adoptive parents will be hurt.

A name is not important.

People will have a hard time getting used to a new name. When you get married, you'll have to change it anyway.

You're too serious about this adoption thing.

"Why," one friend said, "is a name so important? A name is just a way of us identifying one another."

In my mind, I answered: *A name is roots. It doesn't matter if my father committed crimes; he's my father. He gave me my name; it belongs to me. I want to write and wear my roots every single day, like an old wedding band from an immigrant great-grandparent. I want to belong to a larger, older, scattered hierarchy of Ohrstroms, wherever and whoever they might be.*

I wanted to sever my past with my adoptive parents. I wanted to put distance between me and failure. I wanted the future to be bright, shiny, new, and alive with success, dreams, loves, passions. I wanted my name, the name my parents gave me, because it belonged to me.

By the time I reached the county court, a sweat stain had formed a blotch between my shoulder blades, and sweat ran off my face. It didn't matter. I felt righteous and strong. I walked into the court chamber and told the clerk I was late, a fact that had not escaped his attention. He told me it was a slow day, and he led me to another chamber, where Judge Edward and the bailiff sat. No one else stood or sat in the room. I ran my fingers through my hair and sat on one of the pews.

The dais the judge sat upon did not intimidate me this time; then again, I was a couple of feet taller. I felt powerful. He called me to him. I stood a few feet distant so I would not have to crane my neck to see him. Like my grampie, he was round and bald, and wore gold-rimmed glasses. Even with the black robes—the robes were not exactly black; they had accumulated the dusty black that adorns a well-worn garment—he seemed kind. I forced myself to stop looking for shiny spots on the sleeves. When he spoke, his voice was warm.

"Young lady, I see you are here to change your name." There was no trace of a New Hampshire accent.

"Yes, sir," I said, respectfully.

"Can you explain why?"

Certainly I couldn't tell him I wanted to sever the ties with my adoptive parents because my adoptive father had raped me and my adoptive mother had blamed me. I couldn't tell him I wanted dreams to come true and I believed names have power, and if I continued to have the wrong name, I could not have the power I should. I couldn't tell the judge who seemed kind anything, because I didn't trust he had a context to put it in.

"I'd like to carry the name I was born with, sir."

"How do your adoptive parents feel?"

How did my adoptive parents feel? I hadn't asked them, but I knew they'd feel angry and possibly betrayed. However, I did not betray them; I was not the one who insisted we pretend my adoptive mother had given birth to me. They had participated in the big lie started by the Commonwealth of Massachusetts.

Perhaps the judge should have asked me, "How do you think your birth parents will feel?" How would my mother feel if she discovered the daughter taken away for a supposedly "better life" had been molested? How would my father feel if he learned the name he had given me had been stolen and locked away in a safe and buried alive somewhere? How would he feel knowing someone breathed life back into his name?

After a time, I answered the judge, "They want me to do what is best and will make me happy."

It was the first and only time I lied about my adoption. Technically, I told myself, I didn't lie. My adoptive parents were supposed to want me to be happy. However, my intention was to hide the truth. The lie tasted bad as soon as it left my lips, even as I rationalized the judge wouldn't believe the truth about my adoptive parents and how they had treated my brother, sister, and me. But hypocrisy would not help me find my parents. I cannot tell the world (or whatever small part might listen) that adoption is based on hiding the truth and then lie myself.

The judge then asked me about my life, and I told him my educational aspirations. In the fall, I would start school at the University of New Hampshire full-time. He smiled, paternally pleased. He liked me; he wanted to help me.

"I don't see any harm in granting this request," he said. "The papers will be sent to you within the week."

"Thank you, sir." I hesitated. "Sir? Could I, uh, do they, uh, you know, put a gold seal on paper?" I blushed.

He beamed. "I think it can be arranged," he said. "Take care with your studies."

I left the court elated. Several days later, I received a document with a gold seal that stated I was legally Barbara Leigh Ohrstrom.

NO ~~IMPRP~~ ~~THIS~~
CERTIFICATE AUTHORIZED

THE STATE OF NEW HAMPSHIRE

ROCKINGHAM , ss.   COURT OF PROBATE

At a Court of Probate holden at Exeter_____ in
said County, on the twenty-sixth day of June_____ A. D. 19 79

Upon the petition of Barbara Morong_____ of Hampton
in said County, praying to have her name changed to that of Barbara Ohrstrom_____
it was ordered and decreed that the name of the said Barbara Morong_____
be changed to Barbara Ohrstrom_____ in accordance with the laws of the State
of New Hampshire.

A record of said change of name has been duly entered in the docket of the Court of Probate
for said County, under __13053_____ .. and recorded on microfilm_____

Given under my hand and seal of said Court at Exeter_____, in
said County, this twenty-seventh____ day of June_____ A. D. 19 79

Edward J. Howard
Register of Probate

A week later, I moved into a co-op living arrangement with David, Janine, Marti, and James, four friends from Odyssey House. I started working at the Odyssey House School as a tutor and enrolled for one class during the summer session at UNH and three classes in the fall.

Laura, another Odyssey House friend, encouraged me about my

search. Laura pushed me to get close to a staff member named Kristin, because Laura felt Kristin would support my search.

In the rigid, stratified atmosphere of Odyssey House, Kristin stuck out. Her twenty-four years of age seemed ages older and more experienced than my almost nineteen. Kristin was cool and responsible and seemed rebellious. She never arrived late for work, but she often wore a battered green wool hat and brought her dog, Arrow, into the house with her. She was crisp and jaunty, and I liked her the first time I saw her bounce in through the double glass doors with her hat and dog. Yet I was slightly afraid of her—what if I didn't measure up? I wanted her to accept me, but I was afraid that if I got close, she wouldn't. So I did a dance, hanging around when I knew she'd show up but never deliberately seeking her out.

Laura thought I was utterly ridiculous. Kris seemed utterly detached. Then Laura and I got instructions to go to New York Odyssey House to attend a special therapy group, and Leslie, another staff member, and Kris got elected to drive us. On the way to New York, we listened to Dan Fogelberg (the first time I heard him), smoked a zillion cigarettes, stopped and had lousy coffee at a bunch of highway dives, and told jokes. Leslie and Kristin wore cool clothes, had cool music, and didn't look down on Laura and me because we didn't.

I can still hear those lyrics by Dan Fogelberg.

You better change/Before the sun goes down/... Better raise your fortresses/ Or tear them down .../Tear them down/Tear them down.

By the time we hit FDR Drive, we were singing these lyrics at the top of our lungs into the traffic around us. To me, these questions shadowed my life. What if the gold of finding my parents poisoned me?

After the therapy group, Laura and I hung out in the street, waiting for Kris to come back. "Come on, Barbara! Stand in the street and let me take your picture!"

I stood in the street.

"Barbara, there's a car coming up behind you!"

"Screw the car!" I gestured with my hand, and Laura caught me on film, half laughing, half defiant, with my finger in the air and my other hand extended with a cigarette.

Kris eventually returned, and we got ready for the long return drive. Kristin drove, and Leslie and Laura fell asleep. Kristin and I talked.

We talked about adoption, about why I had to know.

Kristin said, "So you always knew you were adopted?"

"I remember *getting* adopted when I was five," I said.

"What do you remember?"

"I remember I skinned my knee on the escalator on the way there. I remember people's knees from standing on the subway—so many people on the train. I remember the judge on a dais with a big podium in front of him. And he called me up, and I remember I had to walk all the way up to him, and it seemed like a long way. When I got there, he looked down at me and asked me how to spell my middle name."

"When did you decide to search?"

"I didn't. I just always knew I would."

"Do you remember your parents?"

"Nope, I don't remember anything. But I used to have this dream I was at the bottom of a flight of stairs, and this woman in white stood at the top—you know, in a white dress. And she reached out her hand for me, and I started up the stairs, reaching out, but as soon as we almost, almost touched, I would wake up."

Kristin didn't say anything.

I continued, "I don't remember a single day where I didn't think about them, wonder what happened, where they were."

"Do you think you want to know them because your adoptive parents hurt you?"

"No," I said, "I think I would have wanted to know them no matter what." Then I hesitated. "But maybe." I lit a cigarette. "I don't know. Maybe."

"Are you looking for the family you never had?"

"Yeah," I said slowly, not wanting to admit it even to myself.

"So what happens if you don't find a decent family?"

"I have to know," I said, "one way or the other. I have to know why. Why we got taken away." I fingered the scar on my lower back, the lumps under the skin familiar and comforting. "I have to know about this scar on my back, how it got there," I said.

"What scar?"

"I got this big scar on my back when I was really little, and no one knows how it got there." I did not tell Kris my adoptive mother said my mother had done it, because I didn't believe my adoptive mother. I touched that scar all the time, reaching behind me, feeling the shiny skin and the lumps underneath.

Then Kris asked me about my search, so I brought her up-to-date. I had made a few phone calls. I wasn't sure what to do next, so I did nothing. I told her how Tom had helped me, how I had gotten my hospital records. When we got back to New Hampshire at five o'clock that morning, I knew I'd found an ally.

Meanwhile, in the early part of July, Bill visited me in New Hampshire to say good-bye, because he was moving to the Odyssey House in Utah. I had never seen enough of him since we'd been in Odyssey together, but now it felt like I'd never see him again. We fought—a furious, hard fight—over nothing the night before he left, probably because he was leaving. It reminded me of our fights over our five-minute age difference years earlier.

At five in the morning, he woke me to walk him to the bus station. The early morning air was cool, and the sun had just broken through the horizon. He walked awkwardly, carrying a battered suitcase that held everything he owned. At the bus station, the reddish sunlight made his skin seem golden.

We hugged clumsily, and I walked away quickly, my vision blurred with tears. A half block away, I turned and looked at him. He stood uncertainly, and at that instant, I'd never seen him look so lonesome or handsome, with one hand holding the suitcase and the other hand shielding his eyes as he looked for the bus.

The bus materialized. Its bulk blackened the low sun, and I turned quickly, before Bill boarded it, and walked. Behind me, I heard the bus driver shift into gear, and the bus bore down on me. At the last second, I turned and waved, but I couldn't see Bill anywhere. I shuffled down the street. The bus and then the sound of the bus faded into the distance.

As I walked, I remembered a time when we were four, and he created an adventure out of our usual nightly bath. The claw-footed tub had overflowed with stuff wondrous to children: bubble bath. Our foster sister had left the bathroom, and Bill and I clambered out of the tub. We examined the blue box, stenciled with imaginary bubbles. Distracting us from the box, a lightning bolt cracked electric blue; we pressed ourselves against the cool dark windowpane and watched the drops glide away on the other side, quickly replaced by more. As he tugged at the wooden frame, forcing it open, Bill's eyes had gleamed. We giggled at his idea to pour bubble bath into the storm, at the fantasy of countless bubbles floating in the night. When we poured out the bubble bath, the powder hissed out of sight, swallowed by the black wetness. Puzzlement gripped us—where did the bubbles go?

I smiled. That was Bill. Then I remembered another, colder afternoon when we were eleven or twelve. Bill, Sue, our older sister, and I had been skating one afternoon on the lake near our house. Carefree as ever, Bill skated close to a dangerously flawed section of ice near a small waterfall. I opened my mouth to warn him, but the ice interrupted with a splintering crack, followed by black water welling over the edges of the hole into which Bill had sunk. Racing toward him, screaming for Sue, I stopped a few yards in front of the gap, warily eyeing the ice. Seconds later, Sue approached in a shower of ice chips as I stripped off my coat and eased myself belly-down onto the ice. Sue lay behind me, clutching my legs, and I inched forward, tossing him my coat. We pulled him out slowly, inching backward by wriggling like snakes in the grass, until the three of us were safe. Then Sue and I threw my coat around him and rushed him home.

That was Bill, too—the risk taker. How I would miss him.

Later that day, I opened the quarterly ALMA newsletter, which advertised a book named *The Reg Niles Searchbook for Adult Adoptees*. I ordered it. It came a few days later, full of addresses of possible places where records existed. I sat, drafted a letter asking for information, and sent it to eighty addresses:

July 18, 1979
Odyssey House
Hampton, NH

To Whom It May Concern:

My name is Barbara Ohrstrom. I am eighteen years old, and presently attend college and work in a library. My reason for writing to you is in hopes you may be able to help me find someone. I am adopted, and the person I am looking for is my natural father. I am not looking for him to place any demands on him, or take anything away from him. I want to find him so I can know what happened the first two years of my life, and just to see what he looks like. I will give you all I know about him in the hopes you know where he is or was located.

His name is William Francis Ohrstrom. He was born in Worcester, Massachusetts, 1930 or 1931. He was thirty years of age as of August 6, 1960. He lived at 161 Williams Avenue, Wareham, Massachusetts, in 1960. He was employed at Surrey Room, Wareham, as a bartender. He was married to a Joan Morris (my mother) in or before 1960. This is all I know about him.

I would appreciate so much if there is anything else you know about this man. This is very important to me; I can't begin to say how important. You can write to me at the above address. *Anything* you know would be helpful. Thank you.

Sincerely yours,
Barbara Ohrstrom

I sent this letter to embassies, federal agencies, drivers' license bureaus, town halls, insurance companies, and other places an individual might leave a paper trail. Not everyone answered; the responses, polite, did not help.

I started calling other places listed in *The Reg Niles Searchbook for Adult Adoptees,* but every time a clerk answered a phone, a small voice inside me would say, "Stop! You're bugging people! Your parents don't want you. You have no right to bother these people." No one, not even Kris, knew I had these secret doubts.

The summer dragged. One night, I went to the library at UNH looking for a book to read and walked into an aisle filled with telephone books. I promptly forgot about reading and spent the night poring through them. I found Ohrstroms in Wisconsin, Oregon, and Massachusetts. Scott Ohrstrom of Wisconsin wrote back to me immediately, drew me an interesting family tree, and concluded I was not related to him. The Ohrstroms listed in Oregon didn't write back. The only Ohrstrom listed in Massachusetts was my "old friend" Valborg, and it scared me to talk to her again.

Possibly related?
Interesting at the least

August 11, 1979
2027 N. Cambridge #4
Milwaukee, Wisconsin

Dear Barbara:

It was nice to recieve your letter - I had thought you probably had decided not to write. Now that you have, I will attempt to fill you in on the Wisconsin branch of the Ohrstrom
family. By the way, I related the gist of our phone conversation to my father, William Gilbert Ohrstrom. He was very
interested because we rarely here from any Ohrstroms other
than our immediate family. Below you will find a rough sketch
of what I know about the Wisconsin Ohrstroms. Should you desire
further information, my Uncle Carl Ohrstrom, has some kind
of book that relates the history of Ogema and describes the
old family homestead. There is a remote possibility that we
are related. The only chance of that would have been if Charles
Oscar (Gustav) Ohrstrom had brothers that like himself had immigrated from Sweden. I have been in Sweden and while I was
there a friend from Stockholm told me that Ohrstrom (which is
not an unusual name in Sweden) was correctly spelled in
Swedish as Årström. Apparently Gustav changed his name to
preserve proper pronunciation.

Charles Oscar (Gustav) OhrsTrom (immigrated from Sweden)
|
Charles OhrsTrom (large logging operation in Ogema which is in Northern Wisconsin.)
Anda
Waldemar } had daughters lives in Philips
Selma
Brenda
Ester
Ella } deceased
Carl OhrsTrom

1887 Charles donated land and
a school to city of Ogema - school
was called the "OhrsTrom School."
1957 school was moved to Price
County Fair Grounds in Philips
Wis. I believe it is a state historical
site. Charles owned large show farm - Very wealthy

Carl James OhrsTrom → my uncle → married Elsie Soukup who Taught in OhrsTrom school
William Gilbert OhrsTrom → my father
|
Scott OhrsTrom — me

over

Without going into too much detail that basically is the
lineage of the Wisconsin Ohrstroms. As I said earlier, should
you desire more information contact my uncle Carl because he
has all the written stuff. His address is below.(he doesn't know
                                         your father however)
You might try contacting the Department of Internal Revenue
or Social Security. I have a friend who was a sometime private
investigator who located missings persons. He said those two
sources usually have information on people unless they are
using assumed names or are dead.

Good luck in locating your father and I hope everything works
out well if you meet him. If you should ever come out to this
part of the country, feel free to look me up.

Scott Ohrstrom

Carl James Ohrstrom
S31 W. 24841 Sunset Dr.
Waukesha, Wisconsin, 53186

But after looking at Valborg's number for a few days, I decided to call her. I sat at the kitchen table and held the phone with one hand, and my head with the other. As soon as she answered, I said, "I called you before. I am William Ohrstrom's daughter Barbara. I am trying to find him because he's my father. Please help me."

Silence, but then, she said, "Yes, I knew your father."

"Do you know where he is now?"

"I raised him," she said. "His parents are dead, and he was in a very bad car accident in 1960." *Maybe the car accident gave me that scar on my back.*

"He was a disgrace to the family."

"What do you mean?"

"There was the car accident in 1960." She wouldn't tell me any more, except to say, "I don't know where he is. Or anyone who would know where he is."

I got off the phone, still scared of her. But why did she keep saying 1960? Did he die and she didn't want to tell me? She seemed like she didn't want to have anything to do with my father or me.

But my life went on. I enrolled in only one class for my fall semester at UNH and kept my job at the Odyssey House School. I also got work as a dishwasher at a restaurant.

And I kept trying. National Look-up, an organization that found people, sent me the names of the neighbors at our house in Wareham, Massachusetts. I wrote to all of them, but none wrote back. I found out the bar where my father had worked was now called the Steakery. Kris drove me down to Barnstable County to see if any records of my parents' divorce or child custody of me existed—nothing.

One cold day in October, I sat in Kristin's office making phone calls. Because she was "junior" staff, she got the coldest, draftiest office on the back porch, with no insulation and very little heat. I worked on the list of town halls on Cape Cod. I asked the clerks to check voter registration lists to see if my parents were still listed on them. Some of the clerks didn't want to, but I usually persuaded them. I called seven or eight places, and decided to quit after one more call because it was close to five o'clock. It's not good to ask a clerk to search near five o'clock. I dialed the town hall in Wellfleet.

"Hello, my name is Barbara Ohrstrom, and I'm calling to see if either William or Joan Ohrstrom appears on your voter registration list." I paused, then continued, "I know it's late and you're busy, but this would help me a lot."

"Who is it you want?" He sounded annoyed, and I instantly regretted I had called so close to five o'clock.

"The last name is Ohrstrom, O-h-r-s-t-r-o-m. First name William or Joan."

"Who are you?"

"Barbara Ohrstrom."

"How come you're looking for them?"

"I'm adopted." After a pause, I continued, "They're my real parents, and I just want to talk with them."

He was silent, and I waited him out. When he spoke, he was blunt and cold. "You're hurting your adoptive parents, and your parents don't want you around."

My cheeks burned with sudden rage. "Voter registration lists are available under the Freedom of Information Act."

"Yeah, you'll have to drive down here and get 'em. I'm not gonna stop what I'm doing and look. You have no right disrupting these people."

"I will drive down! You've got no right hiding my life from me!"

He banged his phone down. I placed my receiver in the cradle carefully; my hands shook. It wasn't my anger or his rudeness that made me stare blindly at the phone while I felt a swell of grief, emptiness, and confusion. I wasn't sure what it was. I sucked in my breath, fighting for control, and Kris walked in.

"Hey, what's the matter with you?" she said gently.

I mumbled and fidgeted. I did not know what was wrong, and I did not want to cry in front of her. But she wasn't about to let me leave the room, and I knew it. I told her about the phone call. She looked at me expectantly, waiting for me to go on. I couldn't. I felt humiliated. This guy had hit my worst doubts. I did not know how to admit I was afraid my mother wouldn't want me and had not wanted me. I needed to believe someone wanted me, but I was afraid no one wanted me. All these thoughts bolted through my mind. I looked at her.

"I can't package up why I'm looking and sell it," I said.

"You're looking for a mother who cares about you," she said.

I started to cry.

She hugged me, and I cried a little bit on her shoulder, but that familiar steel wall inside me emerged, and I backed away from her.

We talked a little bit about searching, and she encouraged me to keep trying. She believed in me, and she believed I had the right to make this search.

I left her office. *I can find my parents*, I told myself.

I have to.

I will.

CHAPTER 2

Agony of Victory

To Whom It May Concern:

My name is Barbara Ohrstrom. I'm writing this letter in hopes you may be able to help me with something I have been struggling with for the past year. I am adopted. I have succeeded in finding my birth and adoption records, but still can't find the whereabouts of my parents. Before I tell you the facts I already know, I will explain the reason I have a need to find my parents. I feel there is a huge gap in my heritage because I don't know my parents. I want to know why I was given up for adoption, and what happened to my parents. I want to just see them, to see what kind of people they are, to find out which one I look like. It's something I think about every day, a part of me I need to fill so I can move on to a full and happy life. I want you to know I don't want to take anything away from my parents or make them feel bad. I just want to know.

At this point in my efforts, I am down to my last resources. It's like taking blind shots in the dark, and I hope something will come back to me—anything. I am a member of ALMA, the Adoptees Liberation

Movement Association. Writing to you is a suggestion from ALMA. Let me give you all of the facts I know concerning my parents and myself, which may aid you in helping me.

My father's name is William Ohrstrom. He was born in Worcester, Massachusetts, in 1930 or 1931. He lived at 161 Williams Avenue, Wareham, Massachusetts, in 1960. He was employed as a bartender at the Surrey Room Bar in Wareham, now called the Steakery. He was married to my mother, Joan A. Morris. He was allegedly in a car accident in Massachusetts in 1960 or around that time period. Both of his parents are dead.

My mother's name is Joan A. Morris, married to my father. She was not employed at the time of my birth. She was born in 1929–30 in Boston, Massachusetts. I have not been able to find anything more about my mother.

My name is Barbara Leigh Ohrstrom. I have a twin brother, Bill, and an elder sister, Sue. My brother and I were born in Wareham, Massachusetts, August 6, 1960. My sister was born in 1959. We were placed in foster care by the Commonwealth of Massachusetts in December 1962. We were adopted by Elwood and Marie Malfide June 30, 1966. The social worker's name was Diane Frost, working for the Commonwealth of Massachusetts.

As you can see, the only two pieces missing are the whereabouts of my parents now, and the facts of my life from birth to 1962.

If there is any way you can help me, I ask you to do so. If there is a fee or if you can forward a letter to my parents for me, please let me know. I will do anything I am able to do to cooperate with you.

Thank you for your time and your consideration of this issue. It's a serious issue, and I know you can disregard it if you choose to. I appreciate deeply anything you can do.

Sincerely yours,

Barbara Leigh Ohrstrom

On Halloween, I mailed eighty of these new letters to more addresses from the *Reg Niles Searchbook for Adult Adoptees*. I was enrolled in a basic composition class at the University of New Hampshire (UNH), worked as a tutor at the Odyssey House School and as a dishwasher at the Galley Hatch Restaurant, and pulled duty (an eight-hour or overnight shift) at Odyssey House once a week.

One year had passed since I sat in the graphics department at Twelfth Street and remembered the incident with *Mr. Ed, The Talking Horse*. The mass mailings from July had garnered results: in the past few months, I learned my father did not register to vote anywhere on Cape Cod, didn't own any property, was not wanted by the FBI, and had not served in any branch of the US military. My parents were married in March 1960 and divorced in 1963.

COPY OF RECORD OF MARRIAGE

DIVISION OF VITAL STATISTICS

RHODE ISLAND STATE DEPARTMENT OF HEALTH

FULL NAME OF GROOM	STATE OF BIRTH	DATE OF BIRTH
William Francis Ohrstrom	Worcester, Mass.	4/2/30
FATHER OF GROOM	FATHER'S BIRTHPLACE	
Hilding E. Ohrstrom	Northampton, Mass.	
MOTHER OF GROOM (Maiden Name)	MOTHER'S BIRTHPLACE	
Grace Magee	Buffalo, N. Y.	
FULL NAME OF BRIDE (Including Maiden Name If Different)	STATE OF BIRTH	DATE OF BIRTH
Joan Audrey Carr (Morris)	Boston, Mass.	10/17/28
FATHER OF BRIDE	FATHER'S BIRTHPLACE	
Thomas W. Morris	Oklahoma	
MOTHER OF BRIDE (Maiden Name)	MOTHER'S BIRTHPLACE	
Kathryn Kemp	Cambridge, Mass.	
NAME OF OFFICIANT	RELIGIOUS DENOMINATION OR TITLE OF OFFICIANT	
Judge William H. McSoley Jr.	Judge 6th Dist. Court	
PLACE OF MARRIAGE		DATE OF MARRIAGE
Cranston , RHODE ISLAND		March 3, 1960

I HEREBY CERTIFY THAT THE FOREGOING IS A TRUE COPY

PLACE WHERE INFORMATION IS FILED	CERTIFICATE NUMBER	FILING DATE
ept. of Records, Cranston , RHODE ISLAND	60-58	March 7, 1960
THIS COPY ISSUED	SIGNATURE OF REGISTRAR	
June 8, 1970	Astrid T. Leidman , City Clerk
cl		

THIS COPY NOT VALID WITHOUT THE OFFICIAL SEAL OF THE ISSUING OFFICE

VS-16A 10M Rev. 68

The fact my parents had been married when Bill and I were born struck me with wonder—I had fallen for the stereotype that mothers who give up their children are alone, poor, young, and desperate, but my mother was in her thirties and married when she gave birth to me and Bill. This indisputable fact comforted me; it gave my mother a solidness and substance … it made her more real to me. However, any information after 1963 remained unreal and beyond my reach. I had no idea where either of my parents lived now.

4:20 p.m., November 2, 1979

I checked my mail; nothing. I left Odyssey House and ran across the street to my dishwashing job. I hated being a dishwasher, but heat, company and free food omforted me. My supervisor, Harry, had sad brown eyes and fine brown hair and elegantly scarred hands. Divorced, with kids, he never allowed the waitresses or chefs to yell at me.

Humming a song I created called "Dishwasher Blues" ("Adoption Blues" would have been a better song for me), I worked alone this day because my dishwashing buddy had gone on vacation. I liked her, but working without her gave me time to daydream and weave elaborate fantasies while the steam rose and soaked my face, arms, and shirt.

I kept trying to imagine growing up with my real parents, but my mind drew blanks. As a child, I had imagined my real mother escorting me through marvelous parks with magical fountains. She had spoken softly to me. Sometimes, she had taken me to museums or symphonies. In these walks and events, her back had faced me, or her head had been tilted. Try as I might, I had never imagined her face.

I had imagined my real father had been a sea captain with a beard and blue eyes, but his face had also been blurred. His actions, however, had not. He had always stormed up the walk and into my adoptive father's house. Sue, Bill, and I had known somehow he was our father. He had seized Al by the collar. "I know what you're doing to my girl," he had said. "I'm taking my kids back right now."

That seemed childish now, but still, I wished I had grown up with them. I wished I could find them and they would be my parents now. I tried to imagine talking to my mother on the telephone about dates or school problems. I tried to imagine my father and mother going to my college graduation or visiting me at college. I wanted my father to be a father who wasn't gross, who wouldn't have touched me when I was a little kid. Thinking about my adoptive father touching me made me squirm inside. I hoped my father would kill him when he learned what my adoptive father had done to me.

I wanted to feel proud of my father. I wanted everybody to watch us if we walked into a restaurant and say to one another, "Look at that father and daughter. Look how much she looks like him, how handsome he is, how good and natural they look together." I wanted to hug him and feel his clean-shaven chin, smell his Old Spice, without flinching. I wanted my father to be my dad.

But that would probably never happen. Maybe he would have made me feel like a nothing, like my adoptive father had. My father wasn't there when I needed him. He wasn't there when Ricky, a neighborhood kid, split my head open with a hammer; he wasn't there when I got A's; and he wasn't there when I learned how to tie my shoes.

But then I pushed my mind in another direction: I imagined finding my parents. I tried to imagine making first contact with them. I'll telephone. No, I'll go to their house and knock on the door. My father will answer. If he asks me how it was, being adopted, I would tell him it sucked. I would tell him—I would tell him I wish he had kept us; God, I wish that so much.

Maybe my father could participate in my life now. He could watch me graduate from college. He could give me away if I got married. He could tell me what happened and why. I'd believe it—it's because of an accident; it's because they didn't have money; it's because they loved us. I'd believe whatever my father tells me.

What if they just didn't give a damn?

They must have! They must have! Why have three kids?

Abortion was illegal, stupid. Birth control wasn't easy to get.

A married couple would not have three kids and give them away and then simply not care.

I ground my teeth. I would not stop searching until they were found; I would not stop because of my cynical fear or other people's beliefs.

Blindly and ferociously, I chiseled the crusted cheese off the onion soup crocks. The steam from the dishwasher rose and stung my face. Furious, I slammed the door shut and felt the salt of tears mingling with the sterile drops of steam. Something had to break soon. I opened the door to the dishwasher, slammed it again, and sang my song. *Come on, kid, loosen up,* I told myself.

I walked to Harry and bummed a Marlboro. We smoked together, and I thought, *what a picture we must make—a sad man and a nutty kid.*

November 11, 1979

I left for school that morning, rushed home, threw my books on my bed, and ran to check my mail. School was already forgotten, and I didn't have to work that night.

Winter was coming, a cold one. I pushed through the front doors of Odyssey House, dashed down the hall, and loped into the staff office. Ah! Mail! A flyer from UNH and two adoption letters. One was a Dear John letter—sorry but. I carefully folded it and tucked it in my back pocket. The second one was from R. L. Polk and Company. They found some Ohrstroms—one in Wisconsin, one in Washington, and, I turned the page, another Ohrstrom in Worcester, William Sr., but he was dead. On the bottom, in blue scrawl, was an Ohrstrom without a first name who lived at 10 Wisteria Street in Salem, Massachusetts.

I clutched the letter. Where was Laura? Where was my pal? She wasn't in the office. I ran upstairs and barged into her bedroom; she wasn't there. I ran downstairs as she entered the front doors, flipping her long blond hair out of her face.

"Laura, come here, quick," I said.

"Wait a minute; I just got in."

"No, no, look. Look!" I shoved the letter at her. "An Ohrstrom in Salem."

"Yeah?"

"Let's go."

"Now? Come on ..."

"It might be my father. Come on. Let's go. I'll get the van keys." I ran into the staff office, grabbed the keys, and signed out. Fifteen minutes later, we had gassed up the van and bought plenty of Marlboros. I steered the white hollow van south onto the highway.

"Hey, Barbara?" Laura said.

"Yeah?"

"You might want to turn on the lights. It's night, remember?"

I switched on the headlights and laughed. We had a longish drive ahead of us. I rambled as I stared at the darkness beyond the windshield. I told Laura I had to go see if this man was my father *now* because I didn't want time to chicken out.

Eventually, we hit Salem. We had never been to Salem, and we didn't bring a map. Salem looked big compared to the small streets and rural highways of Hampton and Exeter. I stopped at a four-way intersection and stared. Cars whizzed by from every direction. Frustration mounted inside me. The intersection seemed impossible to cross.

Laura advised me, "Barbara, go into the first two lanes, and the other two lanes will stop and let you go."

I'm from New Hampshire, I thought, and panicked—I couldn't do that. But I did. We blocked traffic, horns blew, and the other two lanes let us through. We burst out laughing; the tension was broken.

After I drove around some side streets, we landed on Wisteria Street. I parked across the street from number 10. It sure was quiet and dark. We got out, and I lit a match at the mailbox. Yep. Ohrstrom. #10. I knocked hesitantly, then loudly. Nobody was home. I stared at the immobile door, stared at Laura, and wordlessly tramped back to the van, opened the door, sat down, and lit a cigarette.

Laura climbed in and said, "Well, we can just wait 'til they get here."

"Yeah. God, I'm so stupid. I didn't think they wouldn't be home."

A car pulled into the driveway as soon as the words left my lips. We hopped out of the van and walked across the street. The woman turned, and I saw that she was scared. I moved my arms out and away from my body and told her my name.

"Are you Mrs. Ohrstrom?" I asked.

She nodded.

"I'm looking for my father, William Ohrstrom. Do you know anybody by that name?"

"No," she said. "My husband's name is William, but he's too young to be your father."

I exchanged looks with Laura. I showed Mrs. Ohrstrom the letter from R. L. Polk and pointed to the line that stated William Sr. was dead. She couldn't see, so I lit a match for her. She sighed.

"That's my husband's father." She hesitated. "William hasn't talked with any of his family for years. He doesn't know his father is dead." She gave me the phone number and told me to call the following night; William would be there. I thanked her and apologized for scaring her.

As I started up the van, I started thinking. *These Ohrstroms are strange. First Valborg, who wouldn't tell me anything. Now this guy, my uncle, doesn't know his father is dead. What kind of family is this? What kind of man is my father? What if he's a creep?* It hit me in the throat, the guts, the heart. It hurt again. I felt urgent, raw, hungry. Then I felt despair—my uncle won't know where my father is. The despair passed, and I drove out of Salem, suddenly tired. *I'll call my uncle tomorrow.*

NOVEMBER 12, 1979

I felt as if I were on the ragged edge of nowhere. I called my uncle, who told me that his name was Hilding, which means William in Swedish, and he didn't paint a rosy picture of my family. Now age twenty-seven, he had grown up in foster homes and odd places.

My grandfather, William Sr., a Navy man, had married three times. Uncle Hilding knew my father, and he had the same father but a different mother. Uncle Hilding had never met my father because they had been raised by different people. Uncle Hilding had heard stories about my father from Valborg Ohrstrom.

My father had lived with Valborg until he was sixteen. Then he quit school and became a bartender. He lived with his mother and supported her while his father was gone. Uncle Hilding said various relatives had shipped my father around when he was a child. He said William had disappeared for months at a time, leaving my father alone to fend for himself.

Uncle Hilding had a big gap in his knowledge after that. My father's family, such as it was, had disowned him years before, maybe because of a car wreck, and now no one knew where he lived. Valborg had said something vague about that car wreck when I had spoken to her on the phone. Uncle Hilding thought my father might live in California. He told me I was a Swede.

His voice was deep and slow, the way so many big men talk. I liked him. He was the first relative who didn't act like I was a Russian spy. He promised to get some photos from Valborg and send them to me, and we finished the call.

I ran my fingers through my hair thoughtfully. It seemed like many people had dumped my father as a child. On the one hand, walking out on his kids was all he knew. On the other hand, if someone hurts you in a certain way like my father was hurt, it seemed that should be the last thing you would do to your family. I wondered uneasily if my father had dumped us the way he had been dumped.

And this car wreck. Did the car wreck give me the scar on my back? Why would his family disown him over a car accident? Or why would he walk out on his family? A car wreck didn't fit as a reason for being disowned. Maybe in the car accident, he had killed somebody else in the family. But Uncle Hilding would have known if my father killed another family member.

NOVEMBER 16, 1979

I closed my apartment door behind me and sat in the kitchen. The sun streamed in, and I carefully pulled my uncle's letter out of my coat pocket. I hadn't opened it at Odyssey House because I wanted to be alone. The envelope was plain white, with pictures inside. Uncle Hilding's handwriting looked childlike. Mine is too; I smiled a little. I pulled out the letter and photos and laid them on the table.

Hi, Barbara!

Here are the pictures I told you about. I hope this thing comes to a positive conclusion for you however it works out. You may decide to do what I did or you may not; however, it will be what you need to do. I hope we will meet sometime and you will feel free to bang on my door if you're nearby.

Some things about our family that would be good for you to know health-wise. The family history includes stroke, heart disease, and that most American disease: alcoholism. Your grandfather and great-grandfather's names were William and great-grandmother's was Hilma. Well, Good Luck,

Peace,

Uncle Hilding

I refolded the letter. My uncle seemed like a hippie kind of guy—a guy I could talk to.

I shuffled the pictures around the table. My father was a boy, frozen in time. His hair flopped over his forehead. In one of the pictures, he sat on his father's lap, and a grimy calendar announced the date as April 1940. His eyes were shut, and he was grinning. In another picture, he was mowing the lawn with one of those old wooden mowers, grinning again, wearing a white jacket and creased pants. He wore shorts in another picture, and I realized I got my crooked knees from him. In another picture, he was a teenager who had just been confirmed at a Lutheran Church or was leaving choir practice. He wore a simple white robe, and his good looks were easy and visible. He was handsome, with black hair and white teeth and open hands. My brother is the image of him, right down to the reckless look on my father's face.

But my father was just a boy here, a boy. I was older than he was, and I couldn't reconcile the boy in the pictures to the man in my head. This boy was a stranger to me, a stranger—yet his genes created my blood, my life, perhaps my very thoughts. I didn't know who the hell this boy was; I didn't know who my father was.

The same old questions ran like a maddening circus act in my mind. *Why did they give us up? Where the hell was he? Why was the Ohrstrom family so scattered?* The pictures gave me something and showed me I still had nothing. As I stared at the ghostly image of my father, I thought about an Indian superstition: if a person's image is caught on film, the spirit is ruined. Was I invading my father's privacy? What if I was being selfish?

But I had to know. I just had to. It would kill me if I couldn't know.

I picked the pictures up and placed them inside the white sheet of paper.

Then I called my sister Sue. Sue lived in Boston then, on Sunset Street, by Mission Hill. I hesitated before I dialed. Sue and I were not close when we were kids. I had invited her to my high school graduation,

45

and she had sent back the tickets ripped in half because I hadn't invited my adoptive father. Ripped in half. I closed the image out and dialed.

I told her about Uncle Hilding and all I knew; she told me to come and see her. She asked for my foster parents' address; she said she wanted to arrange a dinner with them.

I hung up the phone, picked up the pictures, left the house, and dropped the pictures off at a photo shop. They would blow up the best pair of them for me.

THANKSGIVING, NOVEMBER 22, 1979

Sue and I cooked a turkey, keeping the stuffing in with a stick pin, played chess, and drank wine. Later that evening, I lay on the couch. The yellow light from the streetlamps shone on the wooden polished floors and mesmerized me as my thoughts drifted. Sue had planned dinner with my foster parents for the next evening. I had brought my sister into the most important part of my life; I had some help.

NOVEMBER 25, 1979

The Powers' house was smaller than I remembered. The white paint was intact, but fading. Inside, curtains hung motionless in the dining room. I looked up the carpeted stairway, remembering throwing Mr. Bubbles soap out the window. My chair moved slowly when I pushed it back to sit at the heavy, dark, polished table for dinner. Gladys and William, my foster parents, appeared smaller and older. He sat at the head of the table, silent, and she talked easily, moved quickly, and brought food to the table.

I felt a great expectation of myself—after all, I was the "searcher." I should be eloquent and state my case, but my tongue felt like cement. Gladys began telling stories about our first meeting on December 21, 1962 ...

And suddenly I am under a Christmas tree, the colors a kaleidoscope. I try to talk, and the effort frustrates me, the words stuck; tears start in my eyes at the pain of not speaking ... far away I hear the Beatles singing "I love you yeah, yeah, yeah, I love you yeah, yeah, yeah ...

And then dinner ended. We drank coffee, and Sue's abrupt voice pierced the silence with questions. I became aware of the items I had lost—my parents, my memory, an unscarred back. I said nothing; I was afraid to speak. Finally, I breathed deeply before asking, "Do you know how I got the scar on my back?"

Gladys looked at me and said, "No, they did not tell us that. The social worker wanted to put you in an institution for retarded children because you did not talk or walk, but I took you away from her, and I said, 'We'll just see about that.' You were wearing nothing but a red snowsuit, and you would not budge. I set you under the Christmas tree, and you did not move."

I struggled to absorb this: what did it mean?

Gladys went on, "So I took the snowsuit off, and you were covered with red sores on your back from underneath your arms to the backs of your knees, and I took you to the doctor that night."

"Oh," I said numbly.

"And I put on the medicine he gave me, and rubbed your arms and legs every single day, and pretty soon, you were up and running around with the other kids."

I thought about what would have happened if the social worker had put me in a home for retarded children. I would have acted retarded if I were surrounded by retarded children and treated as if I were retarded. Gladys had saved me.

She was still talking, pointing at the couch. "You used to sit right there with Barbara Gay, and she would read to you all the time. The two of you were very close."

"Was my mother," I suddenly asked, "left-handed?" They didn't remember.

Then Gladys gave Sue a ceramic Santa Claus my mother and father had brought on their only visit together on Christmas 1962.

The evening had flown. We said our good-byes and promised to stay in touch, but the years apart had made us stiff with one another. I didn't know how to act around the Powers because I felt scared and shy.

However, as soon as Sue and I stepped outside, I wanted to run back into their house. What had happened to us? Could anyone tell me what had happened to us? What was missing? But I didn't run back into their house because I didn't know how to ask those questions. It seemed to me the Powers knew more than they had said. Their eyes had said they were sad, even though Gladys had tried her best to act cheery, but they did not say why.

A few days later, in my bathroom, I stared at my eyes in the mirror. My eyes did not seem different, and it seemed they should since I had learned Gladys had kept me from being put in a home for retarded children. I stared into myself and willed memories to return, but they couldn't, they wouldn't, they didn't come.

I had my life, which, according to the Powers, I'd nearly lost. I hadn't been fighting only to talk or walk—I had been fighting for my life. Let the state, I thought in sudden rage, let the state stop me now. I turned out the light, stared at my shadow in the mirror, and walked away.

NOVEMBER 30, 1979

It was unnaturally warm and bright on the UNH campus. I thought about my next step in the search, even though I hadn't let enough time go by on the last round of letters I had mailed. A guy named John Daws of the American Cemetery Association had sent me a wonderful letter. His son was adopted, but Mr. Daws, instead of acting guarded or angry, understood my need to know. He'd sent copies of my letter to a bunch of cemeteries in Massachusetts. I'd received negative responses from these cemeteries. I shrugged. I didn't want any news from a cemetery—why should I get any? My parents had to be alive. They were too young to be dead.

I walked slowly past Hamilton Smith Hall, up a slight hill, and through a parking lot. I saw a little girl, maybe eight years old, illuminated sharply against the shadow of Thompson Hall. She seemed free, pristine, and occupied with something on the ground. I walked near her, and she looked up in sudden fright because she was exposed: a daydreamer. I offered her what I hoped was a gentle and warm smile.

She stared at me in that eternal suspicion children have of adults, and then she surrendered to the part of her that needed warmth and she smiled shyly. I walked by slowly, and when I turned to look back, she was staring at the ground again. I wondered what she saw, what she searched for.

I felt light and full of love, inexplicably. She had pulled me out of my morbid musings, and there was, I reminded myself abruptly, more to live for than my damned obsession with the past. There was the present, my never-ending supply of homework, enjoying the sun, being nineteen years old (which meant I was supposed to have few responsibilities, great sex, cheap beer and food, none of which I had, except responsibilities, and too many of those).

I had to study now, mail to retrieve, work at five o'clock. I walked into the library, which seemed like an old friend since I'd found all those Ohrstroms there. A few hours later, back in Hampton changing into my grubby dishwasher clothes, I decided I had time to get my mail, see Laura, and then run to work. I lit a cigarette confidently in that stupid way to tell everyone cigarettes didn't affect my health, and ran out my apartment door coatless.

The Odyssey House staff office hummed with people, phones, and clattering typewriters. Trying to complete their reports by five o'clock, staff members rushed so they could go home. My mail—only three envelopes—sat forlornly in its little slot. Somebody wanted me to buy life insurance, a flier, which I tossed without reading, and another letter from a cemetery. I opened it and skimmed.

Interred remains ... Joan A. Ohrstrom ... November 1970. I froze.

I reread the letter.

Dear Miss Ohrstrom:
RE: Lot 8100 Grave 162 Bluebell Path

We received a copy of your letter to the American Cemetery Association and have the following information for you:

We have interred at Mount Auburn in the referenced grave the cremated remains of Joan A. Ohrstrom, who was born October 17, 1927, and who died at Cambridge, Massachusetts, on November 25, 1970. The grave in which the remains were interred in was owned by a Thomas Morris of Belmont, and the arrangements were made by a sister of the deceased, Katherine A. Morris ...

The cemetery has no records of any William Ohrstrom.

We trust this information may be of help to you.

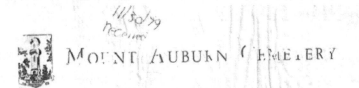

I remained frozen.

I reread the letter. The fact my mother was dead didn't change. "My mother is dead," I said aloud, almost musing, not quite believing, just to try the fact on, see how it felt on my tongue. Everyone in the staff office stopped and looked at me. I walked slowly out of the office.

I walked up the stairs to Laura's bedroom. I felt slow and clumsy and stupid; my tongue wouldn't work when she greeted me, and I looked at her dumbly. She asked me what was wrong, and I said, "My mother is dead."

I sat on her bed with the warm sun touching my back, but I didn't feel it. I didn't feel Laura's hand on my shoulder. I didn't know how to talk. She waited. I handed her the letter. She read it, and she hugged me.

"Talk to me, Barbara. What's happening with you?"

"I have to go to work, Laura; I have to go to work."

She looked at me, and I saw the pity in her face directed at some other person unrelated to me.

The letter hung limply from my hand, and I looked away from her and stared at the worn floorboards and absently counted them to the door.

She said something, I don't know what; I only half-heard her. I looked at my watch and stood up.

"How can you go to work? You can't go to work." She looked at me helplessly.

"I'm going to work now. I'll see you later; we'll talk later." I left even as she desperately told me to call in sick to work, to tell them there was a death in the family.

Work was lift the racks. Run them through the machine. Scrape the plates. Scrub the pots. My mother is dead. Lift the racks. Run them through the machine. Scrape the plates. My mother is dead. Spray the garbage off the counter.

Finally, at midnight, I sat on two dish racks standing together as the cooks prepared to leave and felt the beginnings of a swamp of grief. I remembered getting lost in a department store when I was five and wandering the impossibly high, long aisles, trying to find my mother.

I wasn't ever going to find my mother now. She was supposed to be there, and now she was gone. I would never see her, speak with her, drink coffee with her, hear what happened, or know why she didn't want us anymore. This time it was permanent. The word tasted unfamiliar on my tongue. Permanent, I whispered. Permanent.

With a start, I realized I must leave. I could not sit there all night; the cooks had already left. I punched out and walked the cool, dark Hampton streets, the streetlights dim in the mist that shrouded them. I felt as muffled as mist; I felt anesthetized.

I wandered and found myself inside Odyssey House. No one disturbed me or even questioned me—I was an "authority figure" there. Some authority I had. I stumbled into the director's office and picked up the phone in the dark and called my counselor, the counselor I used to have in New York, an ex-counselor. I was too young to have ex's. I should have had ex-lovers, maybe, or ex-jobs. Not ex-counselors. Not ex-parents.

The phone burred in the silence. The light from the phone was greenish blue. The voice of my ex-therapist stretched clearly through the wires. "Why are you calling so late?"

Oh yeah, I told myself, I have to talk now, have to lift myself out of my mind. "Well, I'm okay really." Silence. "My mother is dead."

"How?"

"I don't know." It hadn't occurred to me to wonder yet.

"How'd you find out?"

"Got this letter from a cemetery in Boston. Mt. Auburn Cemetery." I looked at the letter in the glow of the phone. "Cambridge, actually." Another clear and silent pause. I was amazed at how clear everything in the dark office suddenly seemed.

"What did you expect?"

Her words penetrated like slivers of glass. I tightened my grip on the phone, exhaled the breath I didn't know I was holding, and felt my mouth open and shut helplessly, like a tadpole gasping for air. It passed. I was swathed in numbness again. I nodded wearily, although she couldn't see it, whispered, "Good night," and placed the phone down gently, although I could've crushed it in one hand. I sat in the dark for a long time, watched the mist swirl outside, watched the letter that wouldn't vanish.

The days of the next three weeks blurred like shadows. People talked to me. I replied in monosyllables and, sometimes, not at all. Kristin told the staff members to stop asking about my mother, after James, another staff member, asked me, "Barbara, why are you so upset? You didn't know her."

My friends felt intensely worried, but I didn't feel it.

I only thought disjointedly *my mother is dead*; at the dish-washing machine, *my mother is dead*; in bed late at night, *my mother is dead*; in the kitchen cooking hotdogs, *my mother is dead*; in the staff office getting my mail, *my mother is dead*; during conversations with people, *my mother is dead*.

In December, it occurred to me to go see her grave. Of course, that was what I should do, I told myself, look at the grave. I borrowed the white hollow van and took Marti, one of the Odyssey House seniors, with me. Driving was hell: hot pain knifed through my shoulder blades, the heat in the van didn't work, and my hands stiffened with cold as I gripped the steering wheel.

I found Cambridge in the throes of rush-hour traffic. I drove through Harvard Square, jumbled with construction, and dark narrow streets, realizing futilely I knew nothing about the location of Mt. Auburn Cemetery. The pain in my shoulders spread until I drove like a wounded animal, crouched over the wheel. I swore at the horns beeping at my hesitations, at the endless traffic lights, at the streets that turned and twisted without pattern.

Somehow I landed on Mt. Auburn Street and followed it until I saw a black pike fence. The fence went on and on; Mt. Auburn seemed like the biggest cemetery in the world. I barely saw the gates; I jerked the steering wheel viciously and turned in. The gates were closed. This is the city, I told myself, frustrated beyond rage. Cemeteries close. This isn't New Hampshire, where cemeteries never close and don't have fences and anyone can go in and pay respects or make gravestone rubbings or howl if they want. I grabbed the letter from Mt. Auburn Cemetery, stared at it, then ripped it and threw it on the dirty van floor and ground it under my foot.

I shut the van engine off and realized I had forgotten Marti's presence. I cradled my head over the steering wheel. I needed help. I needed someone who could think clearly about directions, cemetery hours, and how to find a single gravestone in the drifts of graves I'd seen out there; like snowflakes, there were so many of them.

I felt young and unprepared for finding my mother dead, and I wondered if I should have waited. I asked for the seemingly inhuman amount of strength it would take to get me and Marti home. I lifted my head and looked at Marti, who looked scared, and I smiled gently, although I didn't feel gentle. "Let's go home."

She nodded helplessly.

The sky was already a deep, cold blue, and the wind had picked up; night would fall in minutes.

The sky had blackened as only December night skies in New England can by the time we returned. I sat in my kitchen with a hot cup of coffee gripped in my still cold hands. Exhaustion, not only physical, overwhelmed me.

Marti had pieced together and taped the letter from Mt. Auburn Cemetery. Now it sat on the Formica table like a living creature, demanding attention. The fold lines creased deeply, the way lines crease deeply in an old man's face, because I had folded it and refolded it so many times. The question Flo asked bloomed in my mind like a parachute opening: how did my mother die?

I suppressed the question, put the letter in my wallet, and went to bed.

January 4, 1980

The seventies had ended, and I felt elated and sad—my adulthood had arrived. I would be twenty years old that year. The letter from Mt. Auburn Cemetery branded the leather of my wallet. I sat at my battered desk and stared at the cracks in the wall. Then I pulled out the letter. At the bottom of the letter, a name existed: Kathy Matthews of North Reading, Massachusetts, had paid for the funeral. I thought about calling her every day, but the thought frightened me.

Nevertheless, I picked up the phone and called her.

She told me she was my mother's sister's only daughter, which made her my cousin. She taught college, which impressed me—it was nice to know someone in the family was smart. We made small talk about our current lives for fifteen minutes, and all the while, my mind raced ahead. How would I ask the question?

Kathy stopped talking.

I blurted out, "How did my mother die?"

I waited, leaning so far forward I was half over the desk and pressing my palm on the wall. Sweat started to run on my chest, under my arms, down my face. Arrgh! I should have never made this call and stirred up old, bad news that didn't mean anything to anyone except me.

"Your mother and my mother committed suicide," she said, agony and ambivalence tied together. "I'm sorry."

No, no, no, I thought, *it's not her who should feel sorry, it is me; it is me, for unburying this miserable mess.*

She continued, "There's other kids; you have a brother and three sisters in Baltimore—they're named Joseph."

Catch that, my mind cried, while she discussed about how our mothers suffered from mental illness. Finally I thanked her, numbly, and terminated the phone call. *Oh no,* I thought, *oh no, this is a body blow.*

CC-107-

COMMONWEALTH OF MASSACHUSETTS

COUNTY OF MIDDLESEX   CITY OF CAMBRIDGE

The following is a copy from the Record of Deaths in said City:

Record Number, __1514__ Date of Death, __November 25, 1970__

Name of Deceased, __Joan Ohrstrom__

Name of Wife Husband __William Ohrstrom__

Maiden name, (if married, divorced or a widow) _____

Sex, __Female__ Color _____ Condition, __Divorced__
(If other than white)   (Single, married, widowed or divorced)

Age, __40__ years, _____ months, _____ days

Disease or cause of death __Acute Pulmonary Edema A complication of Barbiturate Poisoning__

__Suicide.__

Residence, __197 Auburn   St., Camb.__ Occupation, __LPN__

Place of death, __Cambridge Hospital__ Place of birth, __Cambridge, Mass.__

Name of father, __William Morris__ Birthplace of father, __Oklahoma__

Maiden name of mother __Katherine Kemp__ Birthplace of mother, __Cambridge, Mass.__

Place of burial __Mt. Auburn Cem., Cambridge__

Date of Record __November   27, 1970__

I do hereby certify that the above is a true copy from the Record of deaths in the custody of the City Clerk as
entered in Volume __52__ Folio __59__

In witness whereof, I hereunto set my hand and the seal of said City, this
__30th__ day of __November__
in the year nineteen hundred and __70__

City Clerk

I pounded the desk. I pounded the wall so hard another hairline crack appeared. I should have had my memory erased, should have never begun this crazy damn search. My mother was insane. Why did she have seven kids? Didn't she know how to fight? Now I had a fight even harder because she offed herself, bit the bullet, swallowed the gun, murdered herself. Murdered herself. I put my fist in my mouth and bit my knuckles.

This departure of hers was permanent. I had all these stupid dreams—talking with her, drinking coffee, and asking her for advice about living because I had to ask someone, and I had wanted to ask my mother. Stupid daydreams.

She owed me an explanation of why, of what had happened. Baby pictures. She could have left a letter explaining. A ring. Some precious object, a talisman that had belonged to her. I hated my life. I hated the fierce need inside me that made me do this search. I hated the part of me that had believed events would give me the family to which I had never belonged, the family I needed so much. Then, I felt paralyzed with fear—of what, I didn't know. The tears wouldn't come, couldn't come; I didn't know how to cry.

I could not tell anyone that night. I told Laura the next day, and I started crying, just a little bit. A few tears squeezed past the enormous lump that started in my belly and ended in my throat, and I said, "Laura, I don't have anyone to put on my emergency card in my wallet. If I get killed, no one will know where I belong."

She made a little card with her name and number on it and gave it to me.

I made her promise to cremate me wearing my blue jeans and throw my ashes into the ocean.

JANUARY 11, 1980

The next week Kristin took me to Cambridge to see my mother's grave. After getting a map and directions from the cemetery gatekeeper, we drove on perfect snowy paths through the largest cemetery I had ever seen. Finally, we reached Bluebell Path, and I walked slowly, brushing off snow and looking for grave 162. Cold gripped me despite the brilliant sun, and my hands went numb as I dug through the snow. I dug down to the ground and saw small gravestones set flush into the bare earth.

After a lot of map consulting and counting of graves, I realized that in the place where my mother's marker should have existed, nothing but frozen ground rested under the snow. My mother did not have a headstone, a marker—nothing. Still, I didn't cry, although I felt a terrible grief for my mother because she had died and no one cared to make sure she had a headstone. Cold fingers fumbling, I removed the silver cross I always wore around my neck, dug a hole in the frozen earth with my keys, and buried it. I swore I would put up a headstone for her as soon as I could get the $2,000 or $3,000 dollars it would take—a long time from now.

After January and then February passed, I quit my dishwashing job. One day when Lorraine, a casual friend, came to my apartment to give me a ride to my tutoring job, I still lay in bed at one o'clock in the afternoon. I told her to leave, and she did, after a while. Instantly, I wished she would return, but she didn't.

I attended my classes numbly. I was supposed to be writing a proposal about my past history and future plans in order to graduate from Odyssey House, but I didn't care about that. Kristin had proposed me for graduation in January 1980, after learning of my mother's death. Kristin later told me most of the Odyssey staff had opposed my graduation, but switched votes when she told them they should not penalize me because my mother's death and suicide devastated me, and I needed to look forward to something.

Meanwhile, I stopped going to my writing class because I could not bear to write what I felt. I knew if I did start to write, those feelings would emerge. Then I stopped going to my dishwashing job. I stopped showering and dressing. I stopped getting out of bed except to eat. (The money I had saved in the co-op apartment fund supported me.) The fear of dying, of committing suicide, of failure, consumed me. The fear I would become as ill as my mother haunted me. This continued for about a month, but eventually, I got out of bed and started to do a little at a time.

March came. On a rainy, dark night, I drove the white van at two in the morning to the Spaulding Turnpike Bridge, released the steering wheel, and then guided it with my finger toward the rail. When the van hit, I grabbed the steering wheel, jerked the van back onto the road, and drove off the bridge and onto the shoulder. I put my head on the steering wheel and started to cry, to sob, great tearing sobs.

I wanted to live. I wanted to live. I did not want to be like my mother. I felt more alive than I had in weeks, but still, still, it was not enough. I told no one, not even Laura, what had happened.

APRIL 4, 1980

Spring arrived. At UNH, I explained to my division of continuing education counselor why I had failed my English class; fortunately, in her compassion, she changed the F to an academic withdrawal. I left her office, hungry. I went to the local coffee shop to get some lunch.

I sat at the counter, looked at the pastries in the glass cabinet, and saw the waitress through the other side of the glass between the pastries. She looked as if she were someone's mother, and I started crying and couldn't stop myself; huge gulping sobs left me airless and wordless. I ran to the telephone by the bathroom and called Laura; all I could say was my name, and sob dry choked tears while she talked nonstop. "It's all right, it's all right, it's all right, you're gonna be all right. Just hang onto the phone, just hang on. I love you, everything is okay, it's gonna be okay. It's all over now, it's all over."

Finally, time slowed again; I found my voice and became aware of the people staring at me as they waited by the phone to use the bathroom. I told Laura, "All right, I'm coming home now, I'm coming home." I slept better that night than I had in weeks, and I sensed my heart struggling to heal. Laura told me she talked to one of the Odyssey House psychologists, Eric, and she had requested he conduct a therapy group for me.

Eric scheduled the group for the following Wednesday evening. I never could have asked for help, and I felt secretly grateful to Laura for asking for me. I was terrified, but my terror did not prevent Wednesday night from arriving. Eric, Kristin, Al, Robert, Michael, Paul, David, Janine, and of course, Laura—the members with whom I had traveled through Odyssey House—sat on couches in my favorite room. I loved the windows, the fireplace, and the magnificent Persian rug.

Eric explained Gestalt therapy: people recreated or created scenes about events or people who had traumatized them, and acted out those scenes. It sounded strange, but I said I would try. Eric removed the cushions from the couch and put them on the floor. He took logs out of the fireplace and put them on the cushions, and he took Laura's pocketbook and put it above the logs. He put a blanket over the logs. He brushed off his hands and sat down. "Okay, I want you to imagine this is your mother's deathbed, and this is the last chance you'll get to see her."

Oh no, my mind revolted. Forget it. I looked at his kind brown eyes, hoping for a reprieve. "I can't do that."

"Try it."

"No, I'm too logical to believe it. If I don't believe it, it won't work. I feel stupid."

"Does anyone here think she's stupid if she does this?"

I looked around at a circle of heads shaking. *Great*, I thought. I looked at Laura for help.

Instead, she offered, "Come on, give it a try. You gotta try something."

So I knelt on the floor next to this lumpy blanket, frayed couch cushions, and Laura's pocketbook. I stared.

Eric prompted me, "Come on, Barbara. What would you say to your mother?"

"I don't know. Don't die. Something like that."

"Keep going."

I started mumbling, addressing my mother in the third person. Eric corrected me and told me to address the logs as if they were my mother. *Oh God, I don't feel a thing*, I thought, *I'm doing this wrong. Ten minutes of this should convince Eric this is stupid and we'll go on to something else, something more dignified.* Every time I stopped speaking, Eric prompted me. I mumbled nonsense.

"I'm sorry she's dead."

"I'm sorry you're dead," Eric said.

"I'm sorry you're dead. I'm sorry I didn't get to meet you; I wanted to know what happened, and I don't understand why you killed yourself."

"Say that last sentence again."

"I don't understand why you killed yourself," and something kicked inside me, like a small motorboat revving up; it faded, then revved stronger. The logs disappeared; everyone in the room disappeared, and I talked to my mother.

"I can't believe you're really dead. I can't believe this happened. All I wanted was to know you and find out who I looked like and what happened. I wasn't trying to make you feel guilty for giving us away; I just wanted to know why. I had to know why and what happened to us, that's all. I just wanted somebody to call when things were rough. Everybody's supposed to be able to call their mother, and I just wanted to have somebody, that's all. And how could you have killed yourself? What's the matter with you? That's a disgrace, a disgrace!

"How come you couldn't wait for me to find you? How come you didn't believe in me? You didn't believe I could find you. If you were gonna kill yourself, you could have left something behind so I'd know, I'd know you loved me—something, a letter, a ring, or if you just couldn't hang on, you could have told someone what to do. Why did you have kids if you didn't want us? I waited for you my whole life, my whole life. I waited to find you, and now, so what? How come you quit? You wouldn't want me to quit, would you? Now who's gonna come to my college graduation, and who am I gonna call? I got no one to call. How am I gonna live my life without you?"

I cried for a long, long time.

Like the day I had cried in the restaurant, time slowed, and I became aware of everyone in the room. Laura and Al had tears in their eyes. The couch cushions looked stupid once again. Laura reached out her hand, pulled me off the floor, hugged me, and whispered she was proud of me. I made a silly joke about the couch cushions, and we started laughing.

I hugged everyone else in the room. Eric asked everyone what they thought. People stayed silent, almost as if they had witnessed a religious miracle. Then someone said she had never seen pain like that before. The room lapsed into an awed silence again. The moment broke when Eric and I put the couch back together, and I handed Laura her pocketbook. Sleepy, I wanted to go home and collapse.

However, Eric had other plans. He blindfolded me and told me to stand in the middle of the room. Dumbly, I did so. I felt as trusting as a child. He turned me around a few times, so I was disoriented. He said,

"Barbara, everyone is going to hug you. You're blindfolded, so you don't know who is hugging you; that's as close to unconditional love as we can get. It's not your mother's love, but it is unconditional."

Everyone hugged me, tightly and for a long, long time. I let hands I didn't know move me and grip me. I felt warm and protected. I felt the terrible aloneness leave me for those minutes.

Laura took me upstairs, and I slept in her room that night as if someone had drugged me.

I don't think any of us were quite the same people after that group.

The next morning, I woke late. *It's over.* That was all I could think. The huge wound inside me had lost its fresh fester. I could resume my life. I knew the wound would never leave me, but the worst had passed.

I had spent nearly an entire semester earning average grades at UNH. I needed to raise my grades. I needed to get a new job. I needed to laugh again. I didn't think about the search, and I thought I would let the rest of it drop.

A few days after that group with Eric, I sat in the staff office on a balmy spring day and called Glenn, the director of Odyssey House, Western USA, who also happened to counsel my brother. Although I didn't like him, I figured he should tell Bill that our mother had killed herself so Bill would have immediate support. Glenn promised me he would look after Bill.

Bill called me later that night to tell me he was fine. "It's not like I knew her anyway," he said.

I frowned when I hung up the phone; Bill's reaction didn't make sense to me. However, I realized he might have cut his losses earlier; that is, he may have decided when we were children to let the entire adoption matter drop. At any rate, he promised to let me tell Sue, because I thought I should visit Sue to tell her our mother was dead and had killed herself. I didn't want to tell Sue about our mother, hang up the phone, and leave her alone.

A few weeks later, I jumped on a Greyhound bus and coasted into Boston. Over dinner, I told Sue, but my careful planning was wasted. Bill had told Sue over the phone our mother had killed herself. Sue screamed at me, and every time I tried to explain, she screamed at me again.

"You just had to go and find her, didn't you? She was just an old drunk bitch! You'd think she never heard of birth control! Then you don't even tell me! You knew she was dead in January, and you didn't even tell me! Why couldn't you have left it alone? Why?"

I didn't say anything. What could I say? I stared into the congealed grease on my plate and wished I had a magic carpet so I could fly away. I had planned on staying all weekend, but I left the next morning. Sue … Sue—it sure seemed like she hated me.

As soon as I got home, I called Bill. "What happened?" I asked calmly, although I felt like thunder roiled around inside me.

"What do you mean?"

"How come you told Sue?"

"Well, it wasn't fair that she not know—I mean, you weren't going to tell her for weeks!"

"Bill, I didn't want to tell over the phone, and you promised you would not tell her!"

"You made too much of a big deal of this whole damn thing," Bill said. "There was no reason she had to wait, except the reasons in your mind."

"What's that supposed to mean?"

"Glenn says you're hysterical and you overreact."

"Glenn!" I screamed. "Glenn! Screw Glenn! What does he have to do with anything?"

"See, he's right; you're hysterical right now."

"Bill, you promised. You broke your word."

"Well, I thought about it, and you were overreacting."

"Bill, what the hell's the matter with you? Glenn do all your thinking for you? You can't think for yourself?"

"I'm terminating this conversation," Bill said. "Call me when you can control yourself."

Click. The phone hummed in my ear. I gripped it so hard I thought I'd break it. I hung up the phone and buried my face in my hands. If only I could cry. If only this were not happening. I didn't understand why this nuclear bomb had gone off among the three of us. I slunk around

New Hampshire and decided maybe Sue and Bill would like me again after some time passed.

I finished my semester at school and started my new job as house supervisor at Odyssey House. The job kept me so busy I barely had time to do my laundry. Weeks flew by. I graduated from the program on my twentieth birthday.

I worked hard, I played when I could, and I acted like a pretty normal teenager-just-turned-twenty. A guy I dated drove to Logan Airport, so we could drink Manhattans and watch the planes take off. I went to the beach. I went to a lot of movies. I ate hotdogs and went for late-night drives with Al. Laura went home to Maryland, and Robert to Texas. Janine and David moved to Utah. Kristin quit shortly after that group. Michael returned to school.

And I lived.

CHAPTER 3

Finding the Strength to Stand

AT THE END OF ONE scalding August afternoon, I sat outside on the sun-heated steps outside my apartment and blasted Dan Fogelberg's Phoenix album. The sun felt good on my back. I sipped iced coffee and let myself go into the lyrics.

> I have cried too/I have cried too long/No more sorrow/Got to carry on/Like a phoenix/I have risen from the flames/No more living/Someone else's dreams.

It was time to pick up the search again, I thought. It was time to find my father.

First, I had to get through the adjustments of the next two weeks: my job at Odyssey House would end, I needed a new, part-time job, and college would start. Then I could retrieve the Reg Niles Searchbook and send another letter. On Labor Day weekend, I moved into an apartment on Hampton Beach with a roommate, and started my new job as a waitress at a local coffee shop. Before I had finished unpacking, I had written my letter.

September 5, 1980
12 Atlantic Avenue
Apt. # 1
Hampton Beach, N.H.

To Whom It May Concern:

   I am writing to you in hopes that you may be able to help
me with a difficult problem. Briefly, I do not know the wherabouts
of my father. His stepbrother believes that he may be in Californa.
In the following sentences I will explain my situation as simply as
possible.
   I need to find my father desparately for several reasons. First
of all, my mother, his wife, has passed away, and he does not know.
I need to ask him some questions about my own medical history that
only he can answer. I also would like to know something about my
early childhood and what it was like. I have never seen my father
and I would definitely like to see him once in my life-time, and
if possible start a relationship with him. Because my mother is dead
she cannot answer any of my questions, and he is the only person
that can. My brother, sister, and I were all adopted when we were
very young. Basically, I know everything about my adoption except
his personal part in it. He is my father, I really feel that I
should meet him. That's the story in a tiny nutshell!
   His name is William Francis Ohrstrom. He was born either
April 2, 1930, or April 12, 1930.in Worcestor, Massachusetts.
He may be employed as a bartender. He divorced my mother in 1963
through a Massachusetts court. His family has not heard from him
either in twenty years. Those are the basic facts.
   Again, this is of great importance to me. I have been looking
for a long time now. I intend to keep trying until I find him
because my feelings are so strong.
   I also realize that adoption is a touchy situation to deal
with. Some people advised me to not mention the adoption at all.
I felt that would be dishonest, and not allowing you to make your
judgements as how to handle my letter. So it is in here.
   If you could forward a letter to my father, give me his
address, or any advice I would deeply appreciate it. Anything
you could do would really help a lot. If you need fees to be
paid or need to know anything about me, I'd be glad to help.
   Thank-you for your time.

                                        Sincerely yours,

                                        Barbara Ohrstrom

WRITE TO
DEPT of MOTOR Vehicles
2570 24TH ST
SACRAMento CA 95818

I sent copies of this letter to all the county offices in California, New York, and Massachusetts. I sent it to the FBI, the VA, Social Security, and any other place in the Reg Niles Searchbook that looked remotely likely. I waited. I went for long walks on the beach.

I continued on my walks, morosely kicking sand, and figured out what was wrong with me. I was lonely. My Odyssey House buddies had moved away. My life had dribbled into go to work, go to school, get my mail, go home, and walk into my roommate's various boyfriends in the bathroom in the morning. It didn't seem like this year held any promise. But I loved walking the beach, feeling the sand, smelling the ocean. Finally, I attended college full-time, and I had a job.

Responses to my letter trickled in; my patience wore thin. Social Security told me they could track my father but wouldn't give me the information because he is entitled to his privacy. Damn his privacy! Who was the adult who gave us up, and who was the baby? I wrote to Social Security and asked them to forward a letter to my father. Their response was less than helpful or supportive.

Social Security
Letter Forwarding Service

From: Office of Central Records Operations
Baltimore, Maryland 21235

Miss Barbara Ohrstrom
30 Winnacunnet Place
Hampton, New Hampshire 03842

Refer to: SPP 4213

Date: FEB   1980

We have forwarded your letter as requested. When we forward a letter, we usually send it in care of the employer who most recently reported earnings for the person. However, if the person is receiving benefits under one of the social security programs, we send the letter to the person's home address.

We cannot assure you that the letter will be delivered or that you will receive a reply. In any event, we cannot forward a second letter.

Department of Health, Education, and Welfare
Social Security Administration

SSA-L958 (6-79)
Prior editions may be used until supply is exhausted

SEPTEMBER 29, 1980

I strolled through the Paul Arts Center outdoor courtyard at UNH. I enjoyed the day. The sunlight struck with such clarity that each leaf looked as if it were limned in black. Then a message, like the teletype at the bottom of the television screen, scrolled behind my eyes, in my inner vision. *You will find your father within three days.*

I looked around the courtyard, wondering if I were losing my mind. The courtyard appeared the same. But, I realized, I had had other premonitions, and they had come true. I had known my mother would not have a gravestone before I'd seen her grave. I had known she was in Massachusetts somewhere.

I knew I would find my father within three days.

OCTOBER 1, 1980

Occasionally I visited Odyssey House to kill my loneliness even though I didn't belong there. I hitched a ride with Cheryl one night—she was night supervisor.

One of the new staff members accosted me at the door and asked me what business I had there.

"Smuggling drugs to the residents."

He was ready to call the cops, and I quickly told him I was a CO.

"What's a CO?" he demanded.

"Candidate-Out," I said stiffly.

He looked blank.

I continued, "I graduated from the adult program."

One of the kids spotted me and ran over to say hello, and the moment snapped. I felt morose about his attitude: I'd been gone a little more than a month, and already, I was fading from Odyssey life.

I walked into the staff office and started riffling the pages of the phone book. Again, the premonition I would find my father ran through my head. At six in the evening, I decided to play the information game. I called Massachusetts directory assistance and spoke with an operator, who performed a regional computer check for me to see if any Ohrstroms had telephone listings. Sure enough, she found a Jean.

For once, I was calm when I dialed another stranger's phone number. Jean, my cousin, knew Valborg and did not sound surprised Valborg had been so uncooperative. She offered to call Valborg and discover if she knew the whereabouts of my father. She told me to call her at nine that night for an answer. I hung up the phone. Sweat formed rivulets between my shoulder blades, and I knew this wait would feel like the longest wait of my life.

I'm afraid he's dead. I canceled the thought before it could mushroom any further, and imagined what I would say to him. "Hi, Dad." No. "Hi, William." No. "Mr. Ohrstrom." Stop being silly, I told myself. Just say, "Hi, I'm your kid. Can I meet you? Can I ask you what the hell *happened* in 1962? Can I ask you why my mother is dead? Can you tell me why you left my mother and why you left us?"

Steady, I told myself. *A little bit of temper there.* I found myself wondering if she were left-handed, if I had inherited that from her. There—she did it again, sneaking into my thoughts. How I wanted her! I wanted her to hold me and tell me everything was all right. I put my fingers on the bridge of my nose, closed my eyes, and squeezed.

I stayed in the office and watched the clock crawl until nine. I lit a cigarette and dialed the same phone, from the same desk, and studied the hairline crack I'd left in the wall from the night I called about my mother. This time, when the phone rang, terror ran through me, but fate couldn't pull the same stunt twice, I told myself. Ridiculous fears. Still, my heart beat hard and fast as the phone rang in my ear.

Jean didn't waste any time. "Your father is dead," she said. "A friend of his stopped by Valborg's a few weeks ago and told her."

I groaned from deep in my stomach, through my chest. I was not surprised, because, after all, I had known, hadn't I?

She hesitated, and then plunged through the conversation. "He hadn't talked to Valborg for a long time," she said. "Valborg promised to send you a copy of the death certificate." And then, very gently, she said, "I'm very sorry."

I sucked air into my lungs and gave her my thanks and address. I hung up the phone. A knock boomed on the door. "Go away," I said. "I can't talk to you." I didn't know what to do. *Get help*, I thought. *Get a staff member.* Cheryl, someone whom I did not know well, was the only staff member left that I knew at all. I opened the door and unsteadily walked into the front office.

"Cheryl, come here." My voice sounded cracked and strained.

"I'm running a group," she said, impatient.

"It's an emergency," I said, stupid. Now my voice sounded like it didn't belong to me.

"Come here and tell me what this emergency is," Cheryl said.

I wanted to strangle her; I wasn't sure if I could walk across the carpet in front of all those girls without losing control. But I didn't lose control. I whispered in Cheryl's ear. "My father is dead."

She stood up, canceled the group, gripped my arm, and escorted me out of the room and into the staff office, where she shut the door firmly in a kid's face.

I felt like a prisoner. I didn't trust Cheryl.

She asked me what happened, and I stared at her, mute. I sat on a desk and swung my legs back and forth. She called the new guy, Dick, the head of the program since Eric had gone, and furtively told him my father was dead and I was not talking. She sat opposite me.

Dick arrived in less than fifteen minutes. A remaining part of my brain observed my thoughts starting to jabber ... my father's dead. I'm inane. Inane sounded like an inane word. Where did I pick up a word like that?

Dick stood directly in front of me, jabbering as inanely as the chatter in my skull about how he could be my father now if I wanted a father. He barged right into me and hugged me, and I felt his sweat everywhere and wanted to vomit. I didn't understand why my tongue felt glued to the roof of my mouth, or why what people said or did seemed foolish and far away.

Dick told Cheryl to call Doc Hoc, which set off a round of giggling inside my skull. He had been a fixture of Odyssey House much longer than I had. I'd made a few emergency phone calls to him when a kid got out of hand; apparently, Dick and Cheryl thought I'd lost my mind.

I lit a cigarette and banged my legs into the desk while Cheryl, and then Dick, spoke with Rowen. After the phone call, Cheryl packed me into her car and took me home. I fell into a deep, dreamless sleep. The next morning I went to work at the coffee shop as if nothing had happened.

That night, I went to Odyssey House and brushed a friend's worried look aside casually. "No big deal," I said. "My old man croaked."

"If it's no big deal," she said, "why do you look as if you've seen a ghost?"

I laughed.

"I almost saw a ghost," I said. "I almost saw my father's ghost, but I was too late. No ghost for me."

My friend got mad.

"Your old man didn't croak. Your father died."

"I don't feel anything. I feel numb, that's all. Just numb."

"All right then," she said. "All right."

She hugged me hard, and I felt tears trapped in my throat.

"What am I supposed to do? I don't know what I'm supposed to do."

She hugged me tighter. A day went by. On October 3, I skipped school. The mail came, and I ran out and got it as soon as I heard the mailman bang the mailbox shut. I opened Valborg's letter slowly.

Dear Barbara:

I'm enclosing the document I told you about (plus 2 copies). I've been looking through pictures to see if I had some of your father, but I guess I gave them to my niece. She has promised to see if she has any that you might like. I believe she sent some to your uncle, Hildy; maybe he already shared them with you. None of us would have recent pictures; these would only be your father as a child, but they still might be important to you.

My sister, who died a year and a half ago, had a lot of pictures, but what her husband has done with them, I don't know, but I will check to see if he still has them, and maybe he will let me have them for you. It may take a while, but I will try.

I'm sorry that life has been so hard on you; how tragic that your father had to be so alone when he had children that would have loved him; I'm sure he regretted not knowing you as he was a very kind, lovable person.

*Sincerely,
from your
Aunt Val*

Valborg S. Ohrstrom
80 Elm Street
Shrewsbury, Mass. 01545

Dear Barbara :-

I'm enclosing the document
I told you about (plus 2 copies).
I've been looking thru pictures to
see if I had some of your father
but I guess I gave them to my
niece. She has promised to see if
she has any that you might like.
I believe she sent some to your
uncle, Hildy; maybe he has already
shared them with you. None of us
would have recent pictures, these
would only be your father as a
child, but they still might be
important t you.

My sister who died a year and a half ago had a lot of pictures I know but what her husband has done with them I don't know but I will che- to see if he still has them and maybe he will let me have them for you. It may take a while but I will try.

I'm sorry that life has been so hard on you; how tragic that your father had to be so alone when he had children that would have loved him; I'm sure he regretted not knowing you as he was a very kind, lovable person.

Sincerely
from your
Aunt Val

74

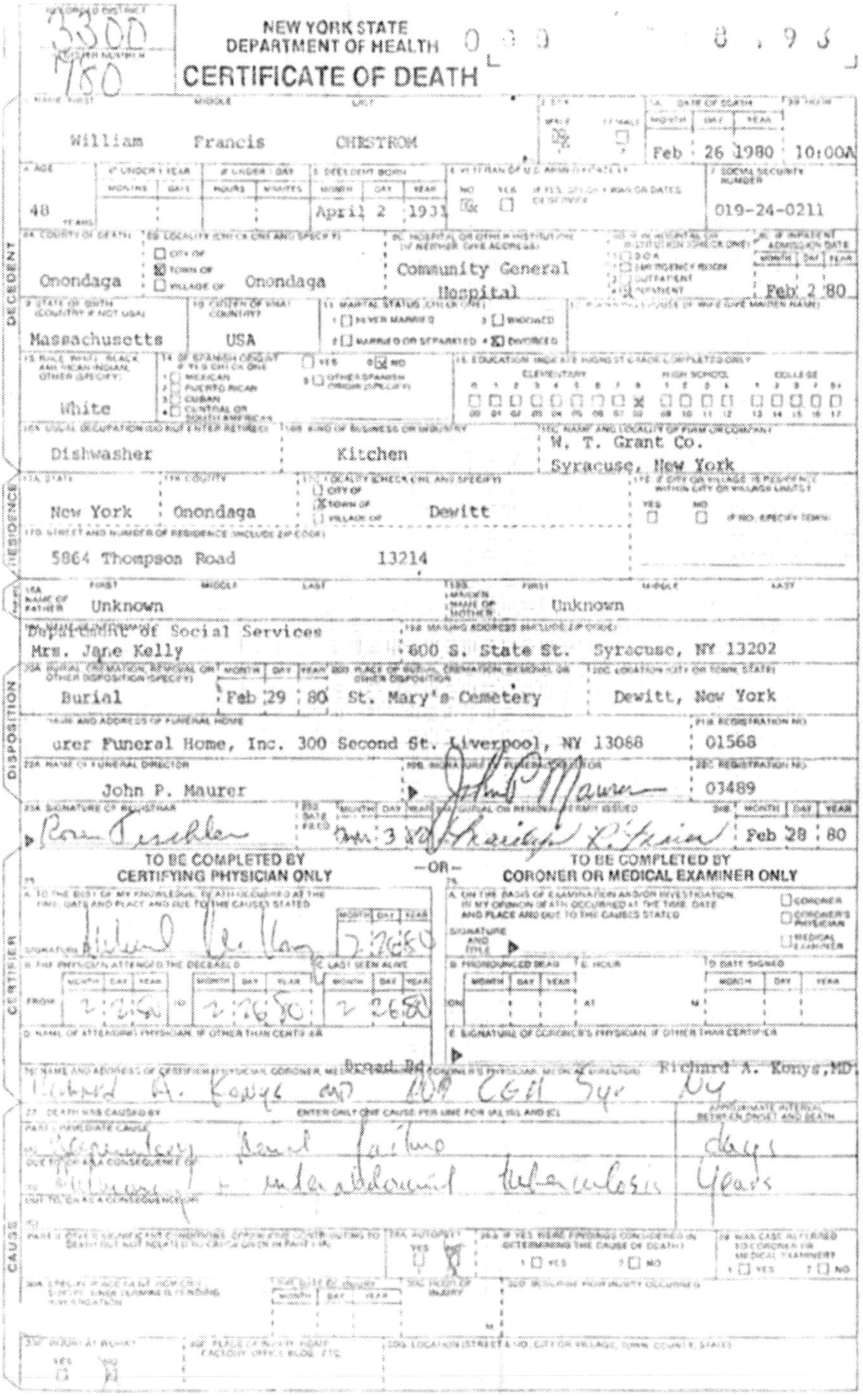

NEW YORK STATE
DEPARTMENT OF HEALTH
CERTIFICATE OF DEATH

3300
780

William Francis OHSTROM

Feb 26 1980 10:00A

48 | April 2 1931 | 019-24-0211

Onondaga | Onondaga | Community General Hospital | Feb 2 80

Massachusetts | USA

White

Dishwasher | Kitchen | W. T. Grant Co. Syracuse, New York

New York | Onondaga | Dewitt

5864 Thompson Road 13214

Unknown | Unknown

Department of Social Services
Mrs. Jane Kelly | 600 S. State St. Syracuse, NY 13202

Burial | Feb 29 80 | St. Mary's Cemetery | Dewitt, New York

urer Funeral Home, Inc. 300 Second St. Liverpool, NY 13088 | 01568

John P. Maurer | 03489

Feb 28 80

TO BE COMPLETED BY CERTIFYING PHYSICIAN ONLY —OR— TO BE COMPLETED BY CORONER OR MEDICAL EXAMINER ONLY

Broad Rd. Richard A. Konys, MD

The last paragraph got me in the throat again; I might have a permanent lump there by the time this search ended. I told myself to breathe as I unfolded the death certificates Aunt Val had sent. My father died of "respiratory neural failure and pulmonary and intra-abdominal tuberculosis."

He died a dishwasher. A dishwasher. *Christ,* I thought, *what happened to tending bar?* He had lived in Dewitt, New York, and worked in Syracuse ... his parents were listed as unknown ... he had an eighth-grade education ... a social worker notified somebody about his death ... and then I read the date of death.

He died February 26, 1980—only seven months earlier. I had visited Manhattan on February 26, 1980 on business for Odyssey House; I had stood in the same state on the same day he had died. I folded the letter, dropped it on the couch, called my friend Pam, an Odyssey House counselor, told her to come to my house immediately, and banged down the phone receiver.

I ran into my bedroom and got my adoption file. I took the *Reg Niles Searchbook for Adult Adoptees* and ripped it apart, page by page, then ripped each page and threw the pieces on the floor. I picked up my adoption file and had it between my hands when the doorbell rang. I let Pam in.

Pages from the *Reg Niles Searchbook* covered the living room floor. I started on the adoption file, and Pam took it out of my hands.

I looked at her wildly. "Seven months! Seven months! I missed him by seven months! I'm gonna blow up the White House! Congress!" I looked at the file. "Give me that!"

She held it away from me.

I ran into my bedroom, grabbed the stack of ALMA newsletters, and began reading captions. "John Doe is fifty and Mom's alive! Susie is forty and Mom's alive. Happy Reunion everybody! Happy Reunion!" I shredded the newsletters and threw the pieces on the living room floor, and then seized the pieces and shredded them again.

Pam somehow got me out of the house and onto the beach. I ran out into the dunes, stumbled, picked myself up, and ran again.

"God," I screamed, up into the sky. "God, You screwed me five times! Five times, God! That's five too many! First I lose my parents! I find my mother dead! I find she killed herself! I find my father dead! He died only seven months ago! It's not funny, God! I'm not laughing! You're a cruel bastard, God! I hope you're getting something out of this! It's not fair! It's not fair! What happened to justice, God? What'd I do in twenty years to deserve this?"

The wind tore the blasphemy out of my mouth and into the waves. I ran and fell and ran and fell and screamed and ran and fell. I didn't care about the few people who heard me, about Pam behind me trying to catch up, about the sacrilege I was committing. Finally, my rage was gone as quickly as it had come. I fell one last time and let the sand grind into my teeth, my nose, my skin, and then I started to cry.

Pam touched my shoulder. "Come on," she said. "Come on, it's cold."

It was cold. It was October on the beach in New England. I snuffled and brushed the sand out of my eyebrows, skin, and hair and walked to my apartment. "Pam, there's no justice in anything, you know that? It just isn't right."

"I know," she said. "I know."

We entered my apartment, and I groaned. Paper shreds covered everything.

"Thanks for taking that file away from me," I said. "I guess I went out of my mind for a minute or two."

"I guess you did," she said.

She stayed, and we talked far into the night. I was confused. Some days I wanted my parents so we could have a picnic and be a family. But maybe if my adoptive parents had been a real family, I wouldn't want these birth parents. Now my birth parents were dead, and my adoptive parents had still treated me like dirt.

I had lost. I felt cheated. Why couldn't I just accept this and move on with my life and not have these feelings?

Bill didn't seem to think our mother's death was a problem. Why did it feel like such a problem to me? Sue said our mother had no sense of responsibility. I didn't feel that way, either. I felt confused, full of grief and anger, and I didn't want to feel that way.

I called work, told them my father had died, and I needed three days off. I got them. I sat around and wrote and moped. It seemed that when people learned I had never known my mother or father, they translated that into meaning their deaths did not matter. They didn't realize that not knowing my parents *and* finding them dead had left me shell-shocked.

I didn't miss the parents I had. I missed the parents I never had. I missed the love it seemed everyone else got from their parents. On school breaks, everyone went home to Mom and Dad. Mom and Dad bailed kids out when they had money troubles. I sat in classes with kids who went home and their moms did their laundry. I felt like I had no one.

Of course, I had to return to work and school. One day, at the financial aid office, a clerk insisted that I must get my parents' signature and tax forms for my aid forms. I told him I couldn't; they were not available. I told him I'd been living independently since I was seventeen. He insisted; it was his job. I sighed. How could I explain I had two sets of parents whom I knew, and one set I still didn't know?

I took the forms from him. I wrote *Parents Deceased* on the section for parental information and returned them to him. He looked at that section, and his face went pale. "Okay," he mumbled, "okay."

I looked him straight in the eye. "Sure you don't want their death certificates?"

"No, no," he said.

I left. *Someday,* I thought as I walked out and let the door slam behind me, *there has to be a way so kids with bad family situations do not have to deal with such nonsense.* It seemed the entire world worked under the assumption everybody had mothers and fathers and a happy homelife, and no one ever died.

I looked in the mirror one evening. I looked too young to have dead parents. I had no lines in my face. I looked like a normal college kid. But I felt like I'd never stop being sad. I hated questions like "Where you going for Christmas?" or "Where are your folks?" I hated forms in doctors' offices: Which family? What health history? I didn't know my parents' medical history, and my adoptive parents didn't count.

My long walks on the beach made me realize how empty I felt. My search had ended. Or had it? Many unanswered questions lingered—where were my missing brothers and sisters Kathy Matthews had told me about? But I didn't feel a strong drive to find them because I didn't think I could handle finding any more dead people.

One night, I dug out pictures of my father again. They looked different. He looked sad. His eyes burned with pain in one picture where his father had his arm around him. My father had sad, frostbitten, hopeless eyes, like he couldn't do anything right and knew it. I saw Bill's eyes in my father's eyes, and I wondered if Bill recognized himself when he saw the copies I had sent him of these pictures.

In November 1980, I rode the Trailways bus to Boston to see Sue again. It seemed like a lifetime had passed since I learned of my father's death, but it had only been one month. Sue still lived on Mission Hill in Boston, and I felt comfort riding the same route on the Arborway Green Line to get to her house. If she was still angry with me, she did not say. I told her our father was dead. She stood and opened another bottle of beer. I told her she could tell Bill. I told her I was exhausted.

I told her what Kathy Matthews had told me ten months earlier—brothers and sisters lived, probably in Baltimore, probably under a name that started with C. I told her I could do no more. Sue said she would take over. We didn't talk much. I felt empty and destroyed. My dream was dead, and I was having trouble adjusting to it. Let someone who was still fresh take on the remaining search. I ate the Thanksgiving turkey, we drank beer, we played chess and she beat me, and I went home. As far as I was concerned, my search was over.

I finally called my old friend Kristin and let her know what had happened. She came to see me at Hampton Beach in December 1980. We went to the local bar late in the afternoon. I sipped a beer and thought abstractedly that I should upgrade my drink. Kris sat next to me on a barstool.

I hadn't seen her for a while; I felt a little stiff, although it made me happy she'd come to see me. She was calm, precise, and logical, and ridden with bleak humor. I didn't know how to convey the anguish I felt. I wanted to appear "fine"; I didn't want to appear "depressed."

Kris put an end to that. "I'm not here because you're fine," she said. "Why don't you tell me why I'm here."

"Things aren't that bad," I said. "I never knew him anyway."

She sat silent for a while.

"That's crap," she said finally. "What are you going to do to fill the hole?"

"What hole?"

"Come on, you can't search anymore—and I remind you that's been your obsession for two years. You had this castle dream. Mom. Dad. Couple of puppies. They'd love you … all that jazz." She gestured cleanly, punctuating her sentences with hand movements.

"It was a great dream," I said. "It could have happened," I said, halfway hearing voices telling me it was impossible, I'd been foolish, I shouldn't have searched.

"But it didn't," she said. "It could have, but it didn't."

"No." I sipped my beer. I stared at the bottles behind the bar. Maybe Jameson's would be a good drink. Johnny Walker Black. Absolut. Tanqueray. I jerked my attention away from the bottles. "I don't want to be cynical, you know? Bitter. I don't want that."

She sighed. "If I were you, I'd be so cynical I'd sell it and make a profit. But you've never been cynical, Barbara. You're a dreamer. You have to find another dream."

I snorted. "I could jump off a bridge."

"Make it a one-foot bridge, okay?" She paused. "You want to go to New York and see his grave?"

"Yes," I said. My voice cracked, and I looked away from her.

She put her arms around me, and as she hugged me, I turned into her and let her hug me. The pain receded to a deeper, more silent place.

"Okay," she said. "Okay, we'll do that. You've got to say good-bye."

Back out on the beach again after Kris left, I dug inside myself to find some hope or optimism to keep me going. I didn't find any. So I started a conversation with God and the crashing waves, and asked for a miracle to make me feel like I wanted to live again.

A day later, Sue called me and asked me to spend Christmas with her. I didn't have other plans, so I agreed. I went to Boston a few days before Christmas.

On Christmas day, we drove to East Andover, New Hampshire, to see Elwood and Marie, the first time I'd seen them in quite some time, and it was hard for me. Christmas day was uneventful, meaning no one fought and Elwood kept his sarcastic comments to a minimum.

I felt depressed and weary; if I hadn't wanted to heal the gap between Sue and me, I would not have come on this trip with her. The New Hampshire winter night closed over Elwood and Marie's house, and it seemed my dead parents' ghosts sighed through the wind and darkness. In a timeless ritual for Sue and me, I began washing the dishes and she began drying them. The phone rang. Marie answered, and called Sue's name. *Probably one of Sue's Boston friends*, I thought, and I stared out into the night again, sightlessly washing a plate.

Sue called me to the telephone. I dried my hands quickly. Perhaps it was Bill wishing me Merry Christmas. I gestured to Sue. "Who is it?" She handed me the phone.

"Hello, Barbara?" It was a southern woman's voice. I frowned and looked at Sue.

"Speaking," I said.

"Barbara, this is Karen, your older sister. I'm just calling you to wish you a Merry Christmas."

I stammered, "You, you're, you—my older sister?"

"Yes. We have a lot to talk about, and I know you can't talk right now. But I wanted to tell you Merry Christmas."

"Merry Christmas," I repeated.

"Okay," Karen said. "Now Sue has my phone number, and I want you to call me when you get home."

"Okay," I said. "I will."

"Good-bye," she said. "I'll be seeing you soon."

"Yes," I said, suddenly fervent. "Yes, you will."

We both hung up the phone. I went back to the kitchen sink, where Sue steadily dried dishes.

"She's pregnant," Sue said. "She's expecting in a few weeks."

"How?"

"Information. Found her right away. Brother Kevin and another sister, Camille. It was easy."

"Did you …"

Sue cut me off. "Let's talk later." She looked at me. "I thought you needed a nice Christmas present."

My eyes filled with tears, and I looked away into the winter night quickly. "Yes," I said. "It's the best present I've ever had."

We finished the dishes. Later that night, after Elwood and Marie fell asleep, Sue told me her story. She didn't have much to add to her cryptic statements over the kitchen sink because she didn't know much more. She had only talked to Karen, and she planned to go to Baltimore next month to meet Karen and Kevin.

Sue had not asked Karen any questions about our mother or our father. It was the first thought that entered my mind, but I realized I needed to ask Karen and Kevin face-to-face. Camille, my other sister, lived in California.

The next day, Sue and I went home, the gap between us closed a little bit. I spoke with Karen on the phone, and planned a trip to Baltimore in March. Karen and Kevin didn't seem real, and they wouldn't, I thought, until I met them. And there was still my father's death, the promise from Kris to see his grave.

JANUARY 6, 1981

I was glad to ring in 1981; 1980 hadn't been a wildly exciting year for me.

Kris, on her way to my place to get me, would drive us to Syracuse, New York, today—my father's burial site. I tried to relax. I admonished myself, *Don't be impatient! Don't look at the clock! Sit down!* I sat on the couch and bounced up and paced.

Come on, Kris! It was 3:02 p.m.; she was two minutes late. *Maybe,* I thought, jittery, *she's not coming. She has a flat tire.* I suspiciously stared at the phone and dared it to ring. The doorbell rang instead.

I pulled the door open, hugged her, and jumped into the car. We were on our way. Several hours later, we edged into western Massachusetts, and the dark clouds started dumping snow. It was a blizzard out there, and out there wasn't that far away—a quarter inch of windshield separated us from the storm. Syracuse was still a hefty distance away, and the snow drove into the car so thickly we were forced to a crawl.

Fragments of memories aimlessly appeared as the snow lunged from the north. I had realized what adoption meant in elementary school, but maybe I'd always be realizing what adoption meant; its meaning, or maybe its impact, seemed to change as I changed. I had always wondered who my parents were and why they had given us up. I had thought my father was a sea captain, that he and my mother had been killed together in a plane crash. Now that I'd found them dead, it seemed I'd never know enough about them.

I smelled fear and realized it came from me. This was the kind of dark storm people die in. The atmosphere of my inner world, the heat inside the car, and the blackness of the space from where the thick flakes came made me feel surreal.

We stopped at a Howard Johnson's for coffee. Inside, it was warm, and people were intimate and suffused with the bond northerners feel when a storm makes them realize how much warmth is worth. Two young men started a conversation with Kris and me. We had exchanged the names of our colleges and swapped cigarettes when one of them asked, "Why are you going to Syracuse?"

That was a normal question. It floored me.

Kris rescued me with a clipped, "Family business."

Back into the storm, more fragments of memory came. "Yes," I found myself answering Jean, "yes, I'm sorry he's dead too; although this also relieves me." Phone calls and mail ceased their monopoly on my priority list. I did not have to run anymore after people who never would move again. I did not have to face the horrible moment of calling a stranger and saying, "Hello, I'm your daughter." Maybe—this thought shocked me—it was easier this way.

I saw a sign for a dumpy motel about twenty miles outside of Syracuse, and we pulled in there and spent the night, relieved to be safe from the storm. In the motel room, I felt like a little kid. Kris breezed past me and dropped her stuff on one of the beds. I had never slept in a motel before. We got some raunchy food, ate in bed, and fell asleep.

The next morning was brilliant, as if the gods wished to redeem themselves for giving us such dangerous weather the day before. The sun blinded and warmed, and streams of melted snow blackened the parking lot. Syracuse was still in the throes of early morning, and the city felt deserted. We drove around and found the cemetery quickly. Slick with icebound potholes and ruts, the driveway wound sharply and stopped abruptly between two buildings. Kris shut off the car engine. I heard nothing; not a car marred the black highway winding above the cemetery.

I spotted a workman and trotted up behind him. Surprised, he wheeled and informed me the attendants (*Attendants? Who are they attending?*) had work in the granite mausoleum. I jogged past him and entered the padded silence of the mausoleum. The aisles were paved with gold carpet, and I recalled a story about Chinese peasants. Poor people rented spaces in buildings like these until they had enough money to properly bury their dead. The atmosphere felt blank, and I knew no one alive was inside this mausoleum.

I stepped outside into the sun. A truck pulled up, and two men got out and entered the house next to the mausoleum. I followed them and entered an office that looked like a gardener's cluttered workshop. After a brief discussion, they told me the location of my father's grave and said my father's grave was next to a grave with the name Button. My father was buried in section 2, shaped like an egg with a broken top, on the outermost semicircle of graves.

I walked over to the section and realized about fifty graves, the headstones buried under yesterday's snow, had to be checked. I dug at the snow with my bare hands. After stumbling through the snow and uncovering about thirty-five headstones, I found Button's grave. I sighed. My hands were red, numb, and covered with tiny cuts where the frozen crystals had lacerated my skin.

I uncovered the next headstone. It was not my father's. Pain flared in my temples. *Oh no*, I thought, *not again*. I stepped back. The distance between the headstones was wrong; a headstone was missing. I fell to my knees. I dug out the headstones surrounding Button's grave—nothing. I dug frantically until I was down to the frozen ground. There was nothing but lumpy, gray grass. I dug more, and pushed the snow in huge handfuls, sobbing air into my lungs. I swore in my head—a litany of obscenity. There was no headstone. No headstone. There was no headstone. I turned and stared at Kris, who stood behind me. The sun had blackened her face. I turned and dug some more. There was nothing but lumps. It was as if he hadn't existed.

I took off my new cross necklace, now almost a year old, warm from the borrowed heat of my flesh. The cross caught the sunlight and dispersed it like a magical thing. *Good-bye*, I thought. *Good-bye*. I dug in the frozen dirt with my house keys, and put the cross in a tiny hole under the sun.

I got off my knees, stood, and turned; Kris turned her head so I would not see the pity in her face. "Let's go," I said. "I'm hungry."

We went to a pancake house, and I devoured a huge stack of pancakes.

"No more death, Kris."

"Okay," she said, agreeable.

"But," I said, "let's go to the funeral home and see if Johnny Undertaker has my father's possessions. A watch or something."

"Okay," she said.

When we got there, Johnny Undertaker was talkative. He didn't have my father's possessions. Apparently a fellow named Martinowsky paid all funeral expenses (except for a headstone) and took my father's belongings. Nope, he couldn't pass on an address for this Martinowsky fellow.

We got into the car, and the snow was brilliant in the morning light. Kris asked me if I wanted to try to locate Martinowsky, and I shook my head. I wanted to go home.

As Kris eased the car onto the highway, I stared out the window. *No matter what else happens*, I thought, *I did the right thing. It's over. I found them. I did what I set out to do, and I know a lot more than I did in the beginning.* That had to mean something. I beat the US government, but nothing could give me the parents I had lost.

I was twenty years old, and it was a big world. *Oh God*, I thought, *please give me a future. Please give me a future without death.*

I watched my burning cigarette's smoke curl out the car window into the blinding whiteness and made up my short adoption wish list. I wanted to meet my new brother and sisters. I wanted to know the woman my mother had been and know the man my father had been.

I turned and looked at Kris. "Got that Dan Fogelberg tape?" I said.

She pushed it into the tape player.

CHAPTER 4

Paperwork and Hearsay: My Mother's and Father's Stories

MARCH 1981

BOSTON

SUE HAD A SURPRISE FOR me: she had arranged a visit with our cousin, Kathy Matthews, the woman who had told me our mother was dead and my brothers and sisters, named Joseph, lived in Baltimore. The next day, we went to Cambridge, where Kathy lived and taught at a college.

Anticipating meeting her petrified me. The day was gray and cold, and we drove around beautiful blocks filled with large trees and classic houses for a while before we found her apartment. I think Sue was scared, too, but she didn't say. I hadn't thought about what I wanted to know: family history, perhaps, or stories and facts about my mother.

Kathy had dark hair and dark eyes. Her eyes looked like I fancied mine did sometimes—a little haunted, marked with grief that would not pass. They had slight rings underneath them. She was pretty, feminine, graceful, and well-dressed. Sue and I were not; we had never learned to dress well, and suddenly, I felt acutely aware of that. We sat in the living room of Kathy's large, comfortable and cluttered apartment. Sue and I sat next to each other on the couch, facing the windows, and Kathy sat in a rocking chair facing us.

Just as when we visited the Powers, I allowed Sue to take charge while I daydreamed a little bit. Then Kathy brought out a box of pictures, and I focused sharply and looked at them. As we looked at the pictures, my mother's story emerged.

My mother's father had left the family after he had been disbarred for embezzlement. He had returned to Oklahoma, his home state, in disgrace. My mother and her sister Sue, Kathy's mother, had been the youngest two children. My mother had been two years old when her father had left, and Sue had been one. The other children, Kenneth, Thomas, and Margaret, had all grown up and left before that happened. Later, they all died.

In the pictures, my mother was dressed in bulky children's clothes. She frequently shielded her face from the camera, and Sue hung onto her in various positions—clutching my mother's hand, her sleeve, the back of her coat. Sue faced the camera more readily. Neither smiled; both looked sad. Their clothes were obviously from the Salvation Army, reminding me of the Salvation Army clothes my sister Sue and I had to wear—smelly old women's coats with itchy, scratchy surfaces and hideous colors. No, Kathy didn't know if my mother had been left-handed, but she knew this: I'm the spitting image of her.

Kathy left gaps, and I did not press her. I think it must be painful to have two strangers ask about intimate details of her mother's life, and I told her this as we left. The pictures were engraved in my memory, and I thought, suddenly, *I don't want to know any more about what happened there.*

When Kathy was fourteen, six months after my mother was found dead in her apartment on Mt. Auburn Street, she pounded on the bedroom door behind which her mother had locked herself. By the time Kathy finally forced open the door, her mother was dead. She could not live with her younger sister, my mother, who was dead. Kathy did not tell me this. My sister Karen did. No wonder, I think, no wonder Kathy Matthews was reluctant to discuss what had gone on with the Ohrstroms, Morrises, Josephs, and Matthews.

A few days later, Sue and I sat inside the Whistling Kettle and blew steam away from our coffee. Across Tremont Street brooded Suffolk County Courthouse, the courthouse in which we had been adopted sixteen years earlier.

"It's easy," Sue said to me. "All you do is walk in, request a hearing, go before the judge—that's it."

I looked at her. She nodded, and we rose as one, put money on the counter, and left.

I paused at the doorway of the old courthouse. My sister looked impatiently at me, and I hurried behind her. Carved wooden banisters and marble floors shone, but the interior was poorly lit and ill-attended. Sue led me through a labyrinth of stairways and corridors until we entered the records room. The records room, also badly lit, was filled with shelves and shelves of yellowed folders that looked sickly under the relentless fluorescent light. A lone clerk, a timeless man, stiffly approached us. My sister tapped her fingers on the counter.

"We're here to get her adoption papers." She jutted her right thumb at me.

A flicker of interest—or was it contempt—crossed his face and died.

"Gotta see the judge," he said.

"I know," she said, impatient.

"Fill this out." He pushed a small rectangular form at me. It was a Records Request Form in triplicate. I filled in my name, date of adoption, and request for adoption records, and signed it.

He took the form, detached his two copies, and pushed the faded pink third carbon back at me; the pink form already looked old.

"Room 32A, 9:00 a.m." he said. "Judge Mahoney." He walked away as stiffly as he had come, and the stacks of records devoured him.

"Thanks," I said, just before he entered the stacks. Sue had already crossed the threshold, and I hurried after her once again.

We reentered the dark, narrow labyrinth and emerged into an

open marble terrace. Room 32A was stenciled neatly across the clouded glass pane of an ancient wooden door. We entered and sat on one of the hard wooden pews.

The judge was missing. A few people sat scattered among the pews—gray-suited men whose faces dully absorbed the lack of light. Mammoth shutters sealed out the natural outdoors light struggling to seep through and illuminate the heavy room. Gravity seemed to press and stoop the shoulders of everyone present. Yellow lights hung high above all of us.

Sue and I sat still, our hands folded neatly in our laps, as if we sat in church. A door creaked, and a male court clerk and Her Honor, Judge Mary Mahoney, entered the room. The judge stepped delicately to the judge's pulpit, and her clerk hastily opened the gate. After Judge Mahoney entered and sat, her clerk closed the gate behind her. Her movements were gracious and deft. She arranged papers on the wooden stand in front of her and looked down at the clerk.

As if prearranged, her clerk began calling cases in a monotone. The first two were not present. I cocked my head, terrified his flat tone would cause me to not recognize my name when he called it. When he called the third case, two gray suits rose simultaneously and approached the judge's area.

Their voices were muted. I relaxed, but within two minutes, the two men walked away, and the clerk's flat tone announced my name. Sue looked at me, and I rose, approached the enclosure around the judge, and looked up at her. She read the papers in front of her, and a stab of electricity went through me when I realized she must have been reading my actual adoption records.

She looked at me sharply, pushing down her reading glasses.

"Good morning," she said.

"Good morning."

"I see you want your adoption records," she said.

"Yes," I said.

"Why?" she asked, looking directly at me. Her eyes were intelligent, bluish-gray, and sharp, but they were not unkind.

"Well, uh, really for principle. I know everything about my real parents already, and I just ..."

She cut me off and waved me to the gate. "Step inside," she said.

I opened the gate cautiously and stepped inside. Now she was not above me.

"Where are your parents?"

"Dead."

She took off her glasses and stared at me.

I continued, "It can't hurt anyone. I know everything anyway." My voice died under her stare. Was it pain or despair I saw cross her face?

She looked away.

"I know what brand of cigarettes my mother smoked," I said gently, my words following her.

Her head jerked, and she looked at me again.

"Parliament," I said.

She looked away again. I waited.

When she finally turned to me for the third time, she said sternly, "Young lady, if I had the time, I would make you tell me how you found this information."

I said nothing.

She seemed disturbed, possibly angry, but not angry at me. "However," she went on, "I don't have time for you today." She sighed. She scribbled something and handed me yellowed pages and the white slip I had filled out in the records room. She had signed her name across the slip and written an illegible word above her signature.

"Take this back to the records room. He'll give you your papers."

She looked away again, and I knew I was dismissed this time.

"Thank you," I said.

She nodded slightly, concentrating on her next case.

I walked away slowly, suddenly drained.

I held my original adoption papers in my hand.

As I walked toward Sue, she rose and stepped in beside me. We exited the courtroom together. Sue stepped ahead of me, but I hesitated and looked at the yellowed pages slowly. I didn't read them; I wanted to absorb them with all my senses. I looked at Sue.

"Could steal them," I said.

"No," she said.

"No," I said. "Just could do it."

"Um hmmm," she said.

I grinned at her, suddenly excited.

She grinned back, a flash of irony electrifying both of us.

"Let's go to the records room," she said.

"Okay."

We retraced our steps and entered the records room. The same timeless man awaited us. He read the judge's scribble, and his eyebrows lifted subtly. He withdrew into the shelves and reappeared a few moments later. He handed me a thin sheaf of photocopies. I glanced at Sue and nodded. I looked at him. He looked at me as if seeing me for the first time.

"Thank you," I said.

"You are welcome," he said.

We left. Through the big doors, the courtyard glowed wetly in the early spring morning sun.

The adoption records consisted of three pages. The first was the Affidavit of the Petitioners, dated May 16, 1966. It noted my adoptive parents' names (Elwood Wilbur Malfide and Marie Dorothy Malfide), address (Route 4, Salisbury, NH), dates of birth (August 21, 1919, and July 13, 1919), occupations (store manager and housewife), ages (46 for both), and the date the adoption took place: June 30, 1966. Yes. I remembered that day.

Elwood and Marie pack us into the car, and we drive through Salisbury, past the state prison, fields, towns, and finally cities, and onto the highway that plunges south to Boston. Elwood pushes the car to a smooth seventy miles per hour, lazily steering with one or two fingers while he smokes with the other hand. At first, I think we are going to visit his family, but Marie says we are going to court to be adopted.

I do not know what adoption means, as I am only five years old. According to Marie, it means she and Elwood are our parents. After Elwood parks the car, we go under the ground to a subway. I have never been on a subway, and hang onto the silver pole with one hand and spin myself around until I make myself dizzy. Elwood grabs my hand; it is time to get off. We arrive at Suffolk County Courthouse in Boston. I am not sure what a courthouse is; if my grampie had come with us, I would have asked him.

There are swarms of people everywhere. Elwood holds my hand tightly as we cross the street and walk underneath a huge gray stone arch. All the people hurry to the same building we do. The building is made of giant stones; the door we walk through is black and as high as our church doors. Inside, it is dark and scary and smells like old newspapers. Grown-ups dash around everywhere, and their shoes click-click on the shiny floor.

We step onto an escalator. At the top of the escalator, I am supposed to step off, but I am scared and do not move. The escalator keeps moving, and I fall onto one knee right where the stairs disappear under the floor. Elwood grabs my arm and pulls me off the escalator. I know he is mad because we are wearing our Sunday clothes, and now I am dirty. He does not say anything to me.

Marie says, "Al, Al, look at her now, look at her now," and points to my knee. My leotards are torn, and my knee is beginning to bleed. He pulls his white handkerchief from his breast pocket and hands it to her silently; she bends and ties it around my knee. When we step into our courtroom for the day, I still sniffle, and Elwood's white handkerchief is red with blood.

The benches we sit on feel harder than the ones in church. A man Marie says is a judge sits behind a shiny wooden rectangle box, and he is much higher than everyone in the room. His robes look like the black robes the minister of our church wears, and the courtroom is drafty and cool, even though it is June outside. I do not understand what is happening. Marie says we are getting adopted, but I don't know what that means either. It must be something like adoption.

Then the judge calls me up in front of his rectangle box, and Marie takes my hand and walks with me up a long aisle with skinny carpet. He rustles papers in front of him, but I can't see or read them. He asks me how I spell my middle name, and, stricken dumb, I look at him. His eyes shoot over my head to Marie, and she explains I did not know how to spell my real middle name, so Grampie taught me to spell it in a way I did know. The judge asks me to spell my middle name, and I say, "L-e-e." (Grampie had taught me to spell my middle name this way.) He nods and smiles, and signs the papers in front of him. Marie turns and leads me to the benches. As we turn, I hear the gavel bang softly.

Later, in the car on the way back to Salisbury, I ask Marie if everyone has more *than one set of parents. She shushes me, and looks at Elwood. We never talk again about that day. We never say the words adoption or adopted after that day. Elwood does not want to hear those words.*

My thoughts were interrupted by Sue insisting, "Barbara? Barbara. Come on, let's get out of here."

Right. I was still in the courthouse, the very same courthouse in which I had been adopted. Sue and I left; she had to run off to work, and I returned to the Whistling Kettle.

After getting another cup of coffee and muffin, I pulled the sheaf out from my leather portfolio case and examined page two. The name Ohrstrom was spelled incorrectly. Hmmm. Courts aren't perfect. The text had typewritten sentences filling in blanks on a standard legal petition form. It said my biological parents were in parts unknown, and in a bit of text that later sent me on the hunt for my mother's psychiatric records, the text said: "Joan Audrey Ohrstrom whose assent is hereby annexed." My mother's signature was annexed? What did that mean? This would bear looking into.

I read further. "It appearing that said child was received by the Department of Public Welfare on September 14, 1962 under the Provisions of General Laws, Chapter 119, Section 23A." Aha. So that was the date we were placed into foster care; that meant we had lived with our parents until just after my second birthday. The state had not gotten involved for two years after our birth, so it had overlooked altering or removing the original hospital records!

Then the record stated something that confused me for quite some time: "consent of and notice to said father is not required on a petition for adoption of said child…" How was that possible? My mother's signature was annexed, but my father's was not required? What had gone on back then? Another mystery—oooh—I hated mysteries; I always had to solve them, one way or another. Clearly, though, this was not the typical adoption that had taken place. Clearly the state had been heavily involved in the machinations that led to our adoption by two unfit parents.

As if to underscore that irony further, the petition text read: "that the petitioners are of sufficient ability to bring up said child and furnish her with suitable nurture ..." Oh, that was rich. Before the adoption, my adoptive father had been married twice to the same alcoholic woman, and bragged about throwing his first son through a plate glass window. He lined us up and beat us with a belt shortly after the adoption had taken place. He had proven vicious, petty, and cruel emotionally and physically in the twelve years I had to live with him.

I turned the page. Ohrstrom was spelled correctly and I was identified as a twin, but otherwise, the information repeated most of the previous page. I sighed. The lengths my adoptive parents, the Department of Public Welfare, and the state of Massachusetts had gone through to keep that information secret from me astounded. I had won a quiet victory over the legacy of sealed adoption records.

True, my victory was painful, but even in the pain, I knew I had pursued exactly the correct course of action. With a bit of luck, perseverance, and intellect, I had defeated all of them. No one but me seemed to know it was a victory even I didn't feel like celebrating. Still, it did feel like a book in my life had been closed, or the circle had been joined, or something like that.

In the meantime, I needed to go to my sister's apartment, get my stuff, and return to New Hampshire. She wasn't the only one with a job and college classes. I wonder if she felt the same as me. Regardless, she had first thought of retrieving adoption records from Suffolk County Courthouse—a powerful idea that gave me this victory.

OHRONO) LEE BARBARA

No. A 3001

ADOPTION AND CHANGE OF NAME.

Barbara Leigh Ohrstrom also known as Barbara Ohrstron

Petition.—Citation.—Decree.

Filed   JUN 9 1986   19

Citation Issued   19

Returnable   19

Allowed   JUN 30 1965   19

Recorded Vol.   Page.

For Petitioner :
John J.Sullivan, Jr. Attorney
Division of Child Guardianship
Department of Public Welfare
600 Washington Street,
Boston, Massachusetts
Tel. No.

For Respondent :

Tel. No.

AFFIDAVIT OF PETITIONERS.

	FATHER		MOTHER	
Full Name	Elwood Wilbur ▮▮▮	Maiden Name	Marie Dorothy ▮▮▮	
		Present Name	Marie Dorothy ▮▮▮	
Residence, No.	Route 4 Street	Residence, No.	Route 4 Street	
City or Town	Salisbury State N. H.	City or Town	Salisbury State N. H.	
Color or Race	White	Color or Race	White	
Age at time of adoption	46 years	Age at time of adoption	46 years	
Place of Birth	Lynn Massachusetts	Place of Birth	Peabody Massachusetts	
	(City or Town) (State or County)		(City or Town) (State or County)	
Date of Birth	August 21, 1919	Date of Birth	July 13, 1919	
Occupation	Self-employed (Store Manager) at time of adoption	Occupation	Housewife at time of adoption	

We hereby request that a certificate of this adoption be sent to the City or Town Clerk of the

.... place of birth of the child.

Elwood _____   _Marie Dorothy_ _____

SUFFOLK, ss.

Subscribed and sworn to this........18th........ day of....May.... 1964

Before me.

.....M. Guy Dole.....   Notary Public.

my commission expires Mar 31 1968

COMMONWEALTH OF MASSACHUSETTS.

SUFFOLK, ss.   At a Probate Court holden at Boston, in and for said County of Suffolk, on the

.... day of

in the year of our Lord one thousand nine hundred and ....

ON the foregoing petition, it appearing that no one appears to consent or object thereto

....

is hereby appointed guardian ad litem of said child, with power to give or withhold consent.

.... Judge of Probate Court.

COMMONWEALTH OF MASSACHUSETTS.

SUFFOLK, ss.   PROBATE COURT.

At a Probate Court held at Boston, in and for said County of Suffolk, on the 30th *day of* June *in the year of our Lord one thousand nine hundred and* sixty-six,

ON the petition of Elwood Wilbur ▮▮▮▮▮

of town Salisbury, XXXXXXXXX New Hampshire,

and Marie Dorothy ▮▮▮▮▮ his wife, praying for leave to adopt Barbara Leigh Ohstrom also called/Barbara Ohstrom a child under the age of twelve years

of William Francis Ohstrom

of parts unknown XXXXXXXXX

and Joan Audrey Ohstrom also called Joan A. Ohstrom his wife, whose assent is herewith annexed
and for a change of said child's name:

It appearing that said child was received by the Department of Public Welfare on September14, 1962 under the Provisions of General Laws, Chapter 119 Section 23A and said Department has since provided for her support and maintenance. Said Department having approved, sponsored and recommended said adoption, it having been assented to by xxxxxxxxxxxxxxx by Robert R. Ott, Commissioner, and a decree was entered in the Suffolk County Probate Court on March 18, 1964 under the Provisions of Chapter 210, Sections 3 and 3A as most recently amended by Chapter 593 of the Acts of 1953 establishing that the consent of and notice to said father is not required on a petition for adoption of said child sponsored by the Department of Public Welfare

and the Court being satisfied of the identity and relations of the persons, and that the petitioners are of sufficient ability to bring up said child and furnish her with suitable nurture and education, having reference to the degree and condition of her parents; and that it is fit and proper that such adoption should take place:

It is DECREED that from this day said child shall, to all legal intents and purposes, be the child of said petitioners, and that her name be changed to that of

Barbara Lee ▮▮▮▮▮

which she shall hereafter bear, and which shall be her legal name.

_____ Judge of Probate Court.

[If the child is under one year of age the consent must be signed before a Notary Public or a Justice of the Peace.]
[A copy of the birth record must be filed. G. L. (Ter. Ed.), c. 210, s-6.]

TO THE HONORABLE THE JUDGES OF THE PROBATE COURT IN AND FOR THE
COUNTY OF SUFFOLK:

RESPECTFULLY represents .... Elwood Wilbur ▓▓▓▓ ....

of ~~Boston~~ Salisbury, New Hampshire , ~~in said County~~ ....

and .. Marie Dorothy ▓▓▓▓ .... his wife, that they are of the age of twenty-one years or (Twin)

upwards, and are desirous of adopting..Barbara Leigh Ohrstrom also known as Barbara Ohrstrom

of .... Boston .... a child of .... William Francis Ohrstrom .... of

.... parts unknown .... , ~~in said County of~~ ....,

and .. Joan Axlray Ohrstrom also known as Joan A. Ohrstrom .... his wife,
whose assent is herewith annexed
which said child was born in .. Wareham in the County of Plymouth ....

on the .... sixth .... day of .... August 19 60;

that ..said child was received by the Department of Public Welfare on September 14,
1962 under the provisions of General Laws, Chapter 119, Section 23A and said
Department has since provided for her support and maintenance. That said child
has resided in the home of your petitioners since June 25, 1965. That a decree
was entered in the Suffolk County Probate Court on March 18, 1964 under the provisions of Chapter 210, Sections 3 and 3A as most recently amended by Chapter 593 of
the Acts of 1953 establishing that the consent of and notice to said father is not
required on a petition for adoption of said child sponsored by the Department of
Public Welfare.

Wherefore they pray for leave to adopt said child, and that her name may be changed to

that of ... . Barbara ▓▓▓▓▓ ....

Dated this .... eighteenth .... day of .... May 19 66

MAILING ADDRESS

.... Route 1 ....

.... Salisbury, New Hampshire ....

▓▓▓▓▓▓▓▓▓▓▓▓▓▓▓▓ .... ▓▓▓▓▓▓▓▓▓▓▓

▓▓▓▓▓▓▓▓▓▓▓▓▓▓▓▓▓▓▓▓

▓▓▓▓▓▓ .... ▓▓▓▓

Elwood Wilbur

Marie Doroth

Consent subster to before me this........................... day of ....

Notary Public.
Justice of the Peace.

I, the child above-named, being above the age of twelve years, hereby consent to the adoption
as above prayed for.

Dated .... June 7, ... 19 66

The foregoing petition is hereby approved and
sponsored by the DEPARTMENT OF PUBLIC WELFARE.

....
COMMISSIONER

Commonwealth of Massachusetts.

Suffolk, ss.   Probate Court.

To ... ... Elwood Wilbur ██████ ... ...

of ..... Salisbury, New Hampshire ....

~~in said County~~, and .... Marie Dorothy ██████ ....

... ... his wife:

....

....

In accordance with Chapter 274 of the Acts of 1957, I certify that

... ... Bunbury, ██████████ ....

of .. Salisbury, New Hampshire ....

~~in the County of~~ ... ...

a child born on the ... 6th ... . day of ..... August ... . 19 60 ...,

was adopted by you on ...... 30th .... day of .... .. June .... 19 66 ....

Signed and sealed this .... 30th ... .day of .. June ...., 19 66 ...

(signature) .... Register.

9-58-2M

St. Patrick's Day, 1981

A New York cabbie dropped me off at Penn Station. Everybody acted as if they or their people came from Ireland, and green beer foam stained napkins, shirts, and party favors. The huge screen inside Penn Station scrolled the arrival of my train, and I moved through a narrow door and down into the concrete bowels and stepped onto the train.

Baltimore. It rolled off the voice in my mind smoothly. I felt comfortable with Karen already from our phone conversation, but I was nervous about meeting Kevin. What if Kevin didn't accept the three new siblings I had thrown into his life? I walked through the cars, rolling with the rhythm of the train. Once I found a window seat, I sat and started thinking, but eventually dozed off. The conductor's voice woke me.

"Baaaaltimore," he cried. "Baaaaltimore."

I got up.

The train inched the last five hundred yards as if it were running out of juice. It seemed we would never arrive, but when we did, I was the first person off the train.

I ran down the train platform and hit the long, ascending stairway two steps at a time. I strained my eyes, looking for faces around the narrow opening of the door. Then I was at the top of the stairs, and I saw a face with wide brown eyes, dark hair, and a shadowed chin studying each face intently. His eyes stopped as he saw me. I knew it was Kevin.

He came near me and shook his head in amazement. "You look just like her," he said, "just like our mother." We stared at each other and walked into the midnight coldness outside.

A cabdriver refused us because Karen's apartment, our destination, was so close, and Kevin told him, "The hell with you." I laughed inside. It was something I would want to say.

We walked together and cussed the cold and the crummy cabdriver.

After five blocks of biting cold, Kevin led me into an apartment building and up two flights of stairs. He stopped in front of a door and beckoned to me. I hesitated and opened the door. It led into a hallway. I stepped through, hesitant again, and walked down the hallway, through another door, and into a warm living room. There were blankets and sheets on the couch, and I smelled their freshness.

The room was pale green, with a heavy dining room table, an easel with a still-life painting on it, an easy chair, paintings stacked against the wall, and hand-built bookshelves. I liked this room.

A woman approached from another hall, carrying a baby. Karen greeted me, and I took my niece, Deana, out of her arms. Deana began to cry, and I shyly handed her back to Karen.

We talked, the three of us. We talked about the Baltimore Orioles, cabdrivers, winter, my uncanny resemblance to our mother, the schools we attended, jobs, and stories about growing up. Karen finally went to bed, but Kevin and I stayed up, talking far into the night. Sometimes, a stillness came, and we both started talking hastily, as if there weren't enough time. Finally I wasn't able to stay awake any longer, and Kevin went home.

I undressed quickly and put on the nightgown Karen had given me. I turned off the light and liked the soft light streaming in through the windows. The room was open and dusky and warm.

I awoke to warmth under my eyelids and the aroma of bacon in my nostrils. The sun and breakfast appeared when I opened my eyes.

After breakfast, Karen brought out a shoe box, and opened it on the table. It was filled with papers and envelopes. She handed them to me slowly. There were cards from our mother. Our mother's funeral announcement. A small black and white photograph of our mother in her nursing uniform that she had sent to Camille in her last letter. She looked serious, a little sad.

She looked like me, and this shocked me. I looked like my mother, down to the curly hair, sweep of my hairline, and premature gray streak that colors my hair. I looked exactly like her—it was as if I stared at a picture of a twin sister.

Deana brought us back to the present with a wail. Then Joe, Karen and Kevin's father, walked into the room and stared at me. His jaw dropped. That's when I realized I looked that much like my mother. Joe embodied my fantasy father. He wore a Navy pea jacket and a captain's hat, blue jeans, and a wide leather belt. I smelled Old Spice as he took my hand and kissed my cheek.

Karen and Kevin told me a lot about our mother's life, and we planned a family reunion for the first week of August—my twenty-first birthday. At that point, Sue was still tracking down Amanda, our youngest sister, and so it looked like our first reunion would have only six of my mother's seven children present.

The family history of the Ohrstroms, Josephs, and Morrises came to me in bits and pieces from various members of the family. Details, caught in my imagination, lost the edge of despair and took on a gleam of romanticism. I could not believe my mother was psychotic. I could believe she was sad and life had done her injustice, and it was so painful she couldn't live anymore. I found it easier to forgive her (as if I had the right to make these judgments) than damn her. She was the only mother I'd ever have. She was it. So she and her sister loved one another, and she just couldn't get past a poverty-stricken childhood. She just couldn't get past her abandonment by my father. The resources available to us now were not available to her then. How could any woman have coped with the loss of two husbands, one boyfriend, and seven children?

As for me, romance was better than villainy, and I couldn't bear to make the only idol I'd ever had into someone wrong. What's more, I still needed her to be just that—an idol of sorts. I could distance myself from my mother's suicide by reasoning resources were available for me; therefore, I'd never end up on the empty end of a barbiturate bottle.

Still, it seemed such a shame, such a waste. I couldn't understand why my mother committed suicide after she had put herself through nursing school and gotten out of the mental institute. The fact she put herself through nursing school proved to me she wasn't psychotic; psychotic people do not graduate from nursing school. I could only imagine my mother died of grief from losing her father, her mother, her husbands, and her children.

Karen and I racked up phone bills and many midnight hours talking of all these things. Karen and I agreed our mother had faced tragedy after tragedy, that her grief must have felt unbearable.

After I read books about the classic traits of an orphan, I understood why I needed to make my mother a hero. But I didn't understand how to stop it—or even why I should. *Let me take my comfort where I may,* I thought—*my mother is dead, and it doesn't matter what really happened. What matters is I need her to be a mother who loved me more than anything else in the world, and that's who she is to me.* When I couldn't believe in God, when I couldn't believe in my family, when I couldn't believe in myself, I believed in my mother. I talked to her in my head, and believe me, she got me through some pretty tough times.

I didn't romanticize my father, Billy Ohrstrom, in the same way, except where his life and my mother's intersected. Originally, the Ohrstroms told me the family held him in disgrace because of a car accident, but that didn't make sense. Clearly, she loved him. Clearly he loved her—but I think he loved her in a different way. I think my father was gay. I think that's why the family held him in disgrace, why he lived in New York, and why a man named John took his personal things from the funeral director.

Nevertheless, the bond between my mother and father was very strong. When she was in Worcester State Hospital, he visited her. When Sue, Bill, and I lived in a foster home, they came together to see us even after their divorce. He granted her the divorce without a fight and surrendered custody of his kids to her.

And when my mother died, Bill Ohrstrom came from New York, stood in Mt. Auburn Cemetery a distance away from the actual grave and mourners, and watched her get put in the ground.

Billy Ohrstrom drank a lot. Kevin remembered seeing him in the bathroom with his pants wrapped around his knees—drunk. My father was handsome and dark and tall. Somehow, I could imagine him and my mother getting along quite well—even when they were fighting. He was something to handle, but she was no slouch either; I'm sure they braced off toe-to-toe many times.

My father felt he could not support us. He couldn't. Between his drinking and the kids, he couldn't make it. My mother also felt bad and complained she didn't want her kids raised in a "fleabag hotel." My mother and her sister always ran to each other in times of trouble, and my mother's sister lived near Worcester at the same time as my mother was bouncing in and out of Worcester State Hospital, just before we kids were sent into foster care. Apparently, Aunt Sue was helping with us kids.

I still hated that my mother was dead. It still brought tears to my eyes, and the tears seemed as if they originated from a bottomless pit and they would always come—at graduations, holidays, weddings, on Mother's day, and nights when I would write about her. My twin, Bill, named this place inside him the void. I named it the void plus pain. Void plus. I could package and sell it.

My mother was, like me, just a woman. She did good deeds and bad deeds. She had tremendous pain. She had been part of the cycle so many members of my family were trying to break: the cycle of child abandonment. Although neither of my parents had an ideal relationship with themselves or each other, it seems they were drawn to what they knew. She said, "Sometimes I get so angry—and I get so angry at myself."

All those shrinks in the sixties—what the hell did they know? They had given my mother drugs. Drugs don't cure pain. The doctors had barely mentioned the trauma of a woman losing seven children, yet other members of the family said my mother had been devastated about it. At least she had known Kevin, Camille, and Karen lived with their father in Baltimore. But my sister Sue, my brother Bill, and me? Hell, somebody from the state had signed us away and made us disappear without my mother's signature. Under a clause in Massachusetts probate law, that mystery about my mother's signature being annexed meant a woman can have her children taken away and adopted without her consent if she is in prison or state custody (such as the custody of a state mental institution).

I never stopped searching for my mother. Oh, I'd put it away and try to forget, but it always came back. She came back demanding vindication. When I was in college, I wrote a rather bad story about a young woman waking up dead and conversing with her mother. It was the conversation I never had with my mother. I lived in Cambridge and poked around all the apartments she lived in. I went to Sarni's and had my clothes dry-cleaned there when I found out my mother had worked there on and off over the years. I tried to get her employment records from Mt. Auburn Hospital. I cajoled Camille into sending me the brief letters and cards my mother had written to her and Karen; Camille typed up the text so it was more compact.

Christmas Card (date unknown)
Dear Camille, I am sending you $5.00 for Xmas. You can either put it in
your bank or spend it. Hope you have a Merry Xmas. Love & kisses XXX OOO
Mommy
Times change, and we with time...But not in the ways of friendship. Wishe
for happiness at Christmas and in the year ahead. Love, Mommy

June 5, 1966 (5 Gilman Street Worcester, Mass)
Since your birthday isn't until August I am writing you a letter. You
will be getting a card from me later.
I do hope everything is fine with you.
Both Kevin and Karen sent me such nice letters and I do want to hear from
you very soon. I am sure you must have a lot to tell me about school and
everything. I bet you are looking forward to your vacation. You certainl
must be getting to be a big girl now.
I hope to be seeing all of you this summer.
I love and miss all of you.
Don't forget be sure and write me.
Lots of Love and Kisses
Mommy

August 6, 1966 Birthday Card (5 Gilman Street Worcester, Mass)
A Birthday Greeting For A Dear Daughter
Happy Birthday Dear
This greeting on your birthday has a specially loving touch
Because you're special, Daughter and you mean so very much!
All My Love
Mommy
Dear Camille,
I do hope you have a very happy birthday. I would love to hear from
you soon. I am enclosing $5.00 for you so that you can get whatever
you really want. I love and miss you very much.
Love and Kisses,
Mommy

December 16, 1966 (address unknown)
Dear Camille,
I received your letter two weeks ago and was very very pleased to hear
from you.
I do hope you will write me often and let me know how everything is.
I am certainly glad that at long last you enjoy school. As long as
you make an effort you should be able to have fun while learning.
How are your marks?--Both Kevin and Karen are playing musical instru-
ments and I suppose you are too. When you write again let me know which
one.
You have very good penmanship for an eight-year old and I am very proud
of you.
I am glad you are well and I too, am feeling fine.
I have moved to 11 Schussler Rd., Worcester. My apartment is very nice
and I can walk to work.
I will be including a money order-this is just like money and Daddy will
be able to cash this for you. Also, there is a nice childrens book store
in Boston and upon my next trip I will buy you a book.
Well, Camille I do hope you have a very Merry Xmas.
I miss you a lot and love you.
Lots of love and kisses
Mommy.

February 4, 1967 (11 Schussler Road, Worcester, Mass)
Dear Camille,
You must have had a very Merry Xmas. I too, had a nice holiday. I got

(cont'd)

gloves, a dress, a nightgown and some nice earrings. I now have pierced ears.
I by now that you recieved your book. I certainly hope you enjoy it. Let me know.
I am proud and pleased that you are doing so very well in school. It really makes school lots easier especially now that you enjoy going. Do keep up the good work.
Things are just about the same here. I am still working at the same job so of course, I have no money problems. I do enjoy my job and I'm feeling well.
I'll be you are looking forward to Valentine's Day. I hope you get a lot of valentines.
By the way I recieved your XMas card. Thanks a lot.
Well Camille, I hope you write soon and let me know how everything is with you.
I love you and miss you.
All My Love
Mommy

October 16, 1967 (19 Crown Street, Worcester, Mass)
Dear Camille,
Just a note to let you know how very happy I was to hear from you again.
I imagine by now you are back in the routine of school. I do hope you still enjoy it. If you have any snapshots I would love to have one from you, Kevin and Karen.
Also if you feel like writing some poetry--I still have your poem.
Please write soon & I will be down to see you over Xmas.
Have Kevin and Karen drop me a note too.
Love & Kisses to all of you,
Mom
See you soon
By the way I have a new address, 19 Crown St that's a nineteen-not fourtee
Love again
Mom

October 28, 1968 (53 May Street, Worcester, Mass)
Dear Camille,
I got your letter and was indeed very happy to hear from you again-I too am sorry that I haven't written more often but my thoughts are with you.
Well, Camille, I enjoyed your poetry very much and I think it shows a grea deal of promise especially from a fifth grader the fact that you enjoy writting poetry speaks for itself. I think its really great that you are planning to write a book and mostly poetry. I certainly hope you will ser me more of your poetry. Don't be dissappointed or discouraged if you can not get your book published. Remember, millions of people (mostly grownup are trying to get there poems published. Any way good luck.
I also would suggest that you read poetry as well as write. I am sure you will enjoy it.
I do hope you like your new school and do not object to being bussed. Thi is also being done in Boston.
I am feeling fine and now work in a hospital. Other than that nothing nev Tell Kevin and Karen I would love to hear from them also.
I miss and love all of you.
Love & Kisses
Mommy
P.S. Have a happy Halloween!

Christmas Card, December 1968 (53 May Street, Worcester, Mass)
For You, Daughter, at Christmas
You've always brought such happiness to those who love you, Dear,
This comes with special wishes Now that Christmas time is here.

(cont'd)

To hope the joy that you have brought will be returned to you
Not only on this Christmas Day but each day all year through.
All My Love,
Mommy
Dear Camille,
Hoping you enjoy your holidays.
I'm enclosing a money order for your Xmas present.
Hoping to hear from you soon.
Love & Kisses
Mommy

January 10, 1969 (53 May Street, Worcester, Mass)
Dear Camille,
Got both your letters within a week and was very pleased to hear from
you again.
I certainly hope that you enjoyed your holidays. I suppose now you are
back in school. You really got good grades in your subjects-keep up the
good work!
Speaking of school, I will be starting my training for nursing Jan 22nd. I
am really looking forward to this. My class will have about 150 students,
ages 17 to 50-quite a variety!
Dont forget if you feel ambitious write some more of your poetry and send
me a few poems OK?
I forgot to mention in my last letter that I got your snapshopts of you
and Karen. How about sending me one (if you have any) of Kevin.
Everything is just about the same here so there just isn't too much to
write about.
I hope your puppy has learned a few more tricks. Dogs can be a lot of fun
I too miss you (Kevin & Karen too) a lot and I think about all of you
often. I certainly will be happy when I can see you again.
All my love & kisses,
Mommy
Write soon!!
Hows the skating coming along?

March 5, 1969 (53 May Street, Worcester, Mass)
Dear Camille,
I got your valentine and was really very very pleased with it. You can
not imagine how wonderful I felt after reading it.
I'm very sorry I did not send all of you valentines.
Anyway I'm glad you had a nice day.
Well between going to school, doing homework and working I've been very
busy.
I really do enjoy school and since many of the students are around my
age, I've made lots of new friends. Homework is sort of a drag-(I never
did my homework in highschool or college). I do study now though since I
would like very much to become a nurse.
We have had snow-snow-and more snow!! We had nearly two feet in one
blizzard not to mention all the hugh drifts. I don't know how much snow
Baltimore has had I hope not as much as Worcester. I honestly will be
very happy when spring comes.
Camille, I have no snapshots of myself but if I can I will stop in Wool-
worths and have a few snapshops made up. If possible I will send them
along with this letter.
How about sending me another picture of you and of Kevin and Karen?
Well there just is no more news but please try and let me hear from you
soon and how you are doing in school etc.
Ask Kevin and Karen to write also.
I really miss all of you and love you.
Love and Kisses
OOOO XXXX
Mommy   (cont'd)

P.S. Again thank you so much for your valentine.

March 30, 1969 (53 May Street, Worcester, Mass)
Dear Camille,
Thanks a lot for sending me the photographs. The one with you, Karen
and Kevin is very nice. I am sending you a couple of snapshots I had
taken in Woolworths.
I also enjoyed your poems about spring.
I hope by now your pen-pal has written you. Don't be too angry with her-
sometimes the longer you postpone answering a letter the more difficult
it is to write. I realize it can be a big disappointment not to recieve
an expected letter.
In regards to your A+ in math-I think sometimes when you don't like a
subject you probably put more time in your studies without being aware
of it.
Everything is just about the same here. I'm doing well in school and
I am still bery busy.
I imagine you are looking forward to Easter and your spring vacation.
Personally I'm looking forward to the vacation!!
Well Camille, I'll say goodby for now.
Give my love to Kevin & Karen and write soon.
Love and Kisses
OOOOOO XXXXXX
Mommy.
P.S. If you have written any more poems, please enclose them.

May 11, 1969 (53 May Street, Worcester, Mass)
Dear Camille,
I enjoyed your poem and your last letter. I guess I'm a little slow
when it comes to answering letters. Something we both have in common.
I'm sorry your friend Sandy is going to move (maybe by now has already
moved). About the only thing I can suggest is that you try and find
another friend or if this is impossible visit with your friends that live
further away if you can. Good luck!!
I am still very busy with my school and work and will honestly be glad
when school is over (another year). I will then have more time to do some
of the things I want to.
I would like to be able to visit you, Karen & Kevin but unfortunately
I can not.
I imagine you are looking forward to your summer vacation.
Do you enjoy baseball games? I used to go to some games when I lived
in Boston but actually I was not all that fond of baseball.
Well Camille I have to do dome homework and get ready for work so will
sign off.
I miss you.
Love and Kisses
Mommy
Please write soon and send another poem.

July 4, 1969 (53 May Street, Worcester, Mass)
Dear Camille
Sorry I was so pokey about answering your last letter. How are you?
I'm fine, like usual.
I imagine you must be on your summer vacation and roasting to death!!
We got our caps in school which means we will be spending the next 10
months at a hospital for our training, rather than at school. I still
will have classes 2 days a week. Next April I will be all through and
will be able to apply for my license. Today, being a holiday was a day
off for me. Eddie and I went to the Cape, went swimming and driving
around the sand dunes, we also went to Provencetown. The dunes are really
beautiful & Provencetown is very quaint and picturous and <u>very</u> artistic.

(cont'd)

A few weeks ago I saw the movie "Popi". This is a movie about two
Puerto Rican boys in New York. It is a movie you, Kev & Karen would
enjoy seeing and if you can should.
I enjoyed your last poem and was pleased you did so well in you Health
Book. Keep the good work up!! Have you read any other good books lately
Well Camille nothing new to write about so will sign off.
Write soon,
All my love and kisses,
Mommy

September 14, 1969 (53 May Street, Worcester, Mass)
Dear Camille,
Well I imagine by now you are back in the routine of school and homework.
I do hope you are enjoying your Spanish. Actually Spanish really is not
too difficult to learn if you just put a little time in it. About the
hardest language to learn is Latin which I imagine you will have in the
future. Since many of the English works are derived from Latin it is
worthwhile learning. Anyway I am sure you will do well in Spanish as
well as your other subjects.
We are in maternity nursing in school and have seen about six films on
childbirth as well as having to learn all the technical details. However
it really is very interesting. Next week I will be working in the nurser
with the new born infants and will be away from homework for a few weeks.
Personally I find homework rather a drag but a necessary evil.
Well Camille nothing new to write about. I have seen some good movies but
a little too mature for you to see.
Give my love to Kevin and Karen.
I miss all of you.
All my love & kisses
OOOOOOOOO XXXXXXXX Mommy
P.S. Write soon.
P.P.S. How about some more poetry?

November 14, 1969 (53 May Street, Worcester, Mass)
Dear Camille,
I'm awfully sorry I took so long to answer your last letter.
I enjoyed your poems very much as usual.
Did you ever change your mind about going out Halloween? I feel that
your teacher was completely ridiculous telling you such tales about
witches etc. Of course there are no people with supernatural powers.
However, there are cultures that belive this and maybe your teacher belon
to one of these groups. Anyway "trick and treating" isn't really all tha
great.
I'm very glad you are doing so well in Spanish but I figured you would
anyway.
We have been having rain, rain and more rain and just about now I'm getti
rather sick of it. Right about now snow is being predicted.
I have less than five months of school left and am looking forward to our
final days. I really have enjoyed it so really I can't complain. We hav
a weeks vacation Dec 28 to Jan 3 and it will be appreciated. You must be
looking forward to the holidays and your vacation.
Well Camille, there just isn't much to write about, but please try and
write soon. I have always enjoyed your letters and poems so much.
Give my love to Kev and Karen.
OOOOOOOOOO
XXXXXXXX   All my love & kisses
Mommy
P.S. Send some snapshots if you have any.

C hristmas Card, December 1969 (53 May Street, Worcester, Mass)
It's so nice to have a daughter like you

109

A daughter like you is a joy and a pleasure. The kind of a girl any
parents would treasure. And if Christmas turns out to be perfect for you,
you'll know that each wish in this greeting came true.
Merry Christmas Honey and a very Happy Year!
Love & Kisses
Mommy
I hope you enjoy your holidays Camille, I will write you a letter very
shortly.
Love again,
Mommy
I am enclosing a money order.

May 11, 1970
Dear Camille,
It's been a long time since I've heard from you and I've really missed
your letters and poems.
I graduated from school April 17, 1970. I have moved to Cambridge, Mass.
This is located just outside of Boston. I will be working in the Cambridg
Hospital as head nurse (3 - 11) in the orthopedic unit. This is where
your fracture patients with broken legs, arms, ribs, heads etc. etc. are.
The pay is fantastic and the hospital is beautiful. All of two years old,
air conditioned and all kinds of electrical devices.
My apartment is tiny but convienient to everything. I can walk to work in
about 5 minutes.
How is everything with you? Are you still enjoying school and doing well.
Most of the colleges up here are protesting (peacefully) and some have
closed down. I can hardly blame these kids. War is a tragic thing and
nothing is ever acomplished by violence. If these wars continue I'm
afraid Kevin will have to face being drafted in a few years. I certainly
hope by the time he is older that all will be peaceful.
Cambridge is loaded with college students and almost all are protesting.
Well Camille, nothing much else to write about so will sign off.
Please write soon.
XXXXXXXXXXX
OOOOOOOOOOO
All my love & kisses
Mommy.

June 7, 1970 (P.O. Box 8745 Boston, Mass)
Dear Camille,
I hope you enjoyed the Art Festival. I do hope you managed to see both
the art and the zoo.
Sorry to hear you had been sick and had to miss school. Speaking of
school you must be anticipating your summer vacation. I certainly hope
you get to go to Wildwood, N.J. Sounds like it would be lots of fun.
I really enjoy my new job. I am usually busy but of course time flys.
I hope in the very near future to be able to get my own furniture and to
be able to decorate my apartment as I would like it. However, all this
takes time.
We have had some very hot weather here and then constant rain. I still
don't like hot weather unless I can get to the ocean.
Well Camille Camille, there just isn't too much to write about.
Drop me a line soon.
Love & Kisses
OOOOOOOOOOOOOOOOO
XXXXXXXXXXXXXXXXX
Mommy

August 7, 1970 Birthday Card (197 Auburn St, Basement Apt., Cambridge, Mas
Daughter-A little bit of sugar, a little bit of spice, a little bit naught

a little bit nice, a little bit owrldly, a little bit wise--add up to a
daughter who's really a prize! Happy birthday Honey!
Love & Kisses
Mommy
Dear Camille,
I am enclosing a check for ten dollars for your birthday. I sincerely
hope you have anice day & get lots of presents (Best part of a birthday)
Well summer is almost over and soon it will be back to school for you.
I've been to the beach a few times, gotten a good tan and managed to cool
off. We have had very hot & humid weather the past few weeks.
I've been very busy at work but I rather enjoy my work anyway.
Not too much to write about. Write soon and include some poetry if you
have the time. Give my love to Kevin & Karen.
All my love & kisses
Mommy
XXXXXXXXXXXXXX
OOOOOOOOOOOOOO
P.O. I've moved to another apartment. Address is on envelope.

September 6, 1970 (197 Auburn St/Basement, Cambridge, Mass)
Dear Camille,
I was very happy to get your poem & report card along with your letter.
I was very pleased with both.
Well by now your back in the routine of school. Let me know what subject
you will be taking. Also, when you get your school picture taken please
send me one .O.K?
Work is about the same. Still very busy.
Did you see the movie "The Out of Towners"? It really was funny & some-
thing you might enjoy. If you are like me when I was your age I went
to the movies every Sat. without fail.
There really just isnt much to write about so will sign sign off. Write s
I love you.
Love & kisses
XXXXXXXXXXX
OOOOOOOOOOO
Mommy

September 22, 1970 (197 Auburn St/Basement, Cambridge, Mass)
Dear Camille,
Got your letter & was very pleased to hear from you so soon. Since I
imagine you are rather anxious to get the information on the eye color
of your grandparents I thought I would answer you promptly.
My mother was of English-Irish descent & had brown eyes. My father was
Scotch-Irish & had blue eyes. This means that I have brown eyes with
recessive blue eye genes and can have blue eyed and brown-eyed children.
It sounds like you are enjoying school this year.
Mario sounds cute & I hope he likes you as well. I'm sure he does. Sur-
prisingly enough the Italians from Sicily are blond and don't even look
Italian.
Speaking of boyfriends can you remember Michael down in Falmouth? The
two of you were all of three years old & it seems you spent more time
over his house than home.
I am enclosing my graduation picture from nursing school. I look sort of
stone-faced.
I truly would like to visit with you, but this decision is you fathers.
Well Camille, I have to go to work so will sign off. Not really much
to write about.
I love you
Love & kisses
Mommy
XXXXXXXXXXXXXX
OOOOOOOOOOOOOO
P.S. Write soon. Give my love to Kevin & Karen.

I deduced from one card that my mother was an empathic person. She wrote she "felt" for the young kids protesting the Vietnam War and hoped the war was over before Kevin was old enough to be drafted. She also felt upset because someone had berated the woman in the room near hers at the hospital.

But her cards were mostly cheerful and typical. She asked Camille to send her poetry. She sent the kids money. She promised to come visit them soon. She commented on the weather. She signed her cards with XXX and OOO's—the universal sign of love.

My mother loved her children. Despite anything else she may or may not have done, her love was undisputable in those briefly written cards. When Amanda, my younger sister, was placed in foster care, my mother went pounding on the door late at night to try to see her.

And then there was Eddy—the man Karen believes was responsible for my mother's death. My mother met Eddy at the mental institution. As family myth has it, and some sketchy records have leaned toward confirming, Eddy worked as an intern at Worcester State Hospital. My mother had a relationship with him. Originally, I thought my mother hoped connecting with Eddy would get her out of the mental institution.

However, just before my mother's death, she moved several times in rapid succession, as if she were trying to lose someone. Was it Eddy? Did she fear him? Or was she trying to escape from someone who could drag her into drinking? These questions can never be answered.

Meanwhile, Eddy went to Baltimore and tried to bribe Joe into telling him my mother's address. Joe told him to go to hell. Whoever my mother was running from, one fact is certain: on November 26, 1970, she couldn't run any farther. She had lost that essential ingredient to life—hope. I can only imagine how much she suffered to end her life after all she had lost—her father, her mother, two husbands, seven small children. She left those seven children, two ex-husbands, and one sister behind.

I still miss her. The wound of losing my mother has never closed. I don't imagine it will.

My mother was tragic; she was responsible. My mother was:

alcoholic, romantic, impulsive, nurturing, smart, self-destructive, left-handed, and beautiful. She smoked Parliaments. She attended nursing school. She worked at Mt. Auburn Hospital. She told Camille to continue to write poetry. I believe she loved all of us. I believe my mother loved me.

I miss my father in a different way. I miss my father when I see paternal men who take their daughters out to dinner, who protect them, who help them navigate the bargaining of buying a car.

I miss the kind of talk family members have—compressed conversations; because they know each other and share so many genetic traits, they can answer each other in a language, a code, known only to them—simple sentences with layers of unspoken meaning.

I poked around and got my parents' divorce records. I reexamined all my papers. I asked my brothers and sisters questions. I read over and over those letters and notes from my mother to Camille and Karen.

It didn't occur to me I still searched. I couldn't control my hunger that would not be satisfied, my cry that could not go unanswered, questions that no one could answer, my ache that would not go away. My feeling of aloneness left me floating in cold, empty, black space, unable to believe any living creature would really stay.

My adoption did not erase my sense of being orphaned or its wounds; my adoption distorted the wound and tried to blot it away.

So how does it all end? It doesn't. I still have those feelings of aloneness and alienation, of floating in cold, black, empty space, insignificant among the stars. I probably always will. However, I have worked to fill my void, find my answers, pray to my God, and be my own hero. I don't have to search for my mother anymore. I don't have to look outside of myself to make my life make sense now. It took me a long, long time to see that, to feel it. Isn't that what all of us must do?

And I have one older brother, one twin brother, three older sisters, and one younger sister, instead of only one twin brother and one older sister. I have seven nieces and one nephew. Best of all, I have myself.

And finally, at last, I have the truth. It's cracked and scarred and tarnished—but it's the truth. It's mine.

MAY–DECEMBER 1988
MIDDLESEX COUNTY PROBATE COURT
CAMBRIDGE, MA

Eight years had passed since the first family reunion. I had graduated from the University of New Hampshire, worked at a publishing house, and graduated from Emerson College. In short, education and hard work had kept me busy. But those missing records between 1960 and 1965 never left the back of my mind. Karen and Kevin had told me our mother, Joan Audrey Morris, had been institutionalized not just once, but many times. Furthermore, I had never heard the complete story of what had happened from Gladys Power and had never retrieved the social work records I knew must exist from our early time as wards of the state of Massachusetts.

These things were on my mind in 1987, and I hired an attorney to see if the original psychiatric hospital records about my mother could be retrieved. The lawyer, unimaginative, had failed to trace the records, stating she could not locate the hospitals in which my mother had been confined.

I had needed to finish my final year in graduate school, so I put the issue aside, and now found myself with a graduate degree and a job at Middlesex County Probate Court.

In a stroke of ironic synchronicity, my supervisor assigned me to work as a clerk, processing guardianships of mentally ill people. This meant I assigned lawyers to indigent clients, filed various petitions for guardianship for mentally ill people, and gained a working knowledge of the state mental health care system in Massachusetts.

The longer I worked at the courthouse, the more impressed I became with Ronnie, one of the assistant registrars of the court. Ronnie had dyed blond hair and wore high heels from the moment she got out of bed in the morning. She was smart, sharp, and knowledgeable about the law. She had worked for the court for years; lawyers routinely sought her advice on complicated estate proceedings. It seemed she knew more law and legal procedures than half the attorneys who came through our section every day. Finally, one day, when the line of lawyers and clerks approaching Ronnie's desk had trickled to zero, I asked Ronnie to help me on my personal matter.

"Oh, that's a tricky one," she said after I had explained what I wanted. "I think you ought to go talk to Marie over in Equity and file it as an equity case."

"An equity case?"

"Yeah. You can argue since other daughters who were not adopted would have access to their mother's hospital records, you should have that same access. Get Marie to tell you how to do it."

So I went over to Equity and talked to Marie, another smart, capable assistant registrar. She listened carefully as I explained the situation, and told me what to write to make my argument.

"What about the fact that I don't know what hospital my mother was in?" I asked.

"Oh, we'll ask the judge to issue an order to all of them, telling them to search their records and turn over what they find. So you have to have all of the hospitals served by the sheriff with your subpoena stating the date of the hearing." Then, she scheduled me for a hearing on November 29, 1988, in front of Judge Mary Manzi, a judge reputed to be tough but fair. And here I had paid an attorney $500.00 when these smart, tough women freely gave me their counsel and help.

First, I had to write the petition, so I wrote a draft and asked Marie to look at it to make sure I had done it properly. She gave me suggestions on fixing it, and I followed them and filed the petition with the court. Then I hired a process server, gave him a list of all state mental hospitals in Massachusetts; the sheriffs served these mental institutions with my subpoena stating a hearing was scheduled to determine if the hospitals would have to turn over any and all records of Joan Audrey Morris they possessed.

The day for the hearing arrived. Standing in front of a judge and trying to explain these adoption and foster care circumstances always unnerved me; I had to try to put into context the very complicated facts of my life in a short, coherent fashion that didn't overwhelm the judge, but didn't deprive her of necessary information. I sat in the courtroom one floor above my office area and waited for the bailiff to call my case.

Judge Manzi sat on a dais, like all the other judges, but the place she directed me to stand while she questioned me seemed closer to her. No one from any of the mental institutions had appeared. She asked me if I understood the request was to grant release of my mother's mental health records. I said, "Yes, Your Honor"; she banged her gavel and said the petition was "allowed."

The order with the judge's signature on it was sent downstairs, where Marie helpfully stamped photocopies with the registrar's seal so I could send the judge's order to each of the mental health institutions in Massachusetts. Because of my work processing guardianships of mentally ill patients, I knew several of the attorneys who worked for the state of Massachusetts and sent copies of the judge's order to the hospitals' legal departments addressed to those attorneys by name.

Still, nearly six months and three thousand miles would pass before those precious records finally reached my hands. By the time the state attorneys did what was necessary to obtain these records, I had moved to San Francisco. The packet from Worcester State Hospital was only a half inch thick; many of the copies were illegible and smeared. Still, I went to a coffeehouse in San Francisco, where I could sit peacefully for a couple of hours, ordered the first of many cups of coffee, and lit the first of many cigarettes. My mother had been hospitalized at Worcester State Hospital (I had thought she was in Westborough) on numerous occasions.

The first page was dated September 17, 1962. (I later learned this was the time period in which my twin brother, sister, and I had been placed in foster care by the Division of Social Services.) It described a suicide attempt: she had taken forty Mellaril tablets and slashed "her left wrist severely with a razor blade. The laceration severed some tendons in her wrist." That was serious. But later on the page came the part that chilled me: "When she was practically in the hospital but still on the street, she then changed her mind and cut her wrists but fortunately she was only a few paces away from the front door of the hospital ..."

I closed my eyes. The scene splashed vividly behind my eyes: the woman, my mother, staggering in the street, groggy from the pills, with blood pouring down her arm; the silver double-bladed razor, red-edged, dropped carelessly into the street. I snapped my eyes open and turned the page.

She had been diagnosed with depressive reaction in an alcoholic personality and placed in the hospital under section 77, which I thought was a mandatory stay for a period of time, as that practice was common in the early sixties. "She is very dramatic in the way she goes from husband to husband (she was already in love with her second husband while still married and pregnant by the first) ..." Hmmm. Her second husband was my father, William Francis Ohrstrom, and if she were married to Joe Joseph, her first husband, and pregnant, that could mean only one thing: Sue was Joe's daughter, not Bill Ohrstrom's as we had thought.

I read on. "The sadomasochistic aspect of her life is ... clear. She torments men until they have no choice but to strike back and inflict injury on her." What? Maybe she was out of control, but it was hard for me to believe she actually tried to get my father or Joe to hit her. Further down the page discussed her relationship with her alcoholic mother, and another line attacked my consciousness: "Shortly after mother died patient experienced a severe depression and attempted suicide." I sighed. Fear crawled down my spine: I did not want to end up like my mother ... and I was terrified I would.

The next page, dated June 5, 1962, was an intake interview taken when my mother was thirty-three and had come to the hospital as an outpatient. "She explained a couple of weeks ago, because of her severe alcoholism and her reaching a point where she thought she might separate from her second husband, she reached the point where she gave up her first three children to her first husband, their father, who is now living in Baltimore." Aha. So that's when Karen, Kevin, and Camille had been sent to go live with Joe Joseph.

They remembered the event and had told me our mother or her sister had called Joe's house, spoken with a babysitter for his second wife's kids, and told her Camille, age four, Karen, age six, and Kevin, age eight, would land at the Baltimore airport in a couple of hours. The babysitter had called the movie theater where Joe and Julie, his second wife, had been watching a film, and had them paged. Joe and Julie had rushed to the airport to meet the kids. My sisters and brother must have been scared! I sighed again.

The report then discussed her education and navy history. She had cut her wrists, had been given an honorable discharge, and had been hospitalized at Boston Psychopathic Hospital for ten days when she was twenty-five. Furthermore, she had attended Boston University for a year, where she met Joe and married him after she discovered she was pregnant.

Her family background stated she was the youngest of five children: her older brother was forty-three (that must be Thomas), a sister forty-one (Margaret), a brother thirty-nine (Kenneth, who later died of muscular dystrophy), and another sister (Katherine, nicknamed Susan because of her brown eyes, like the saying "brown-eyed Susan"). Susan, the sister who had attended to my mother's funeral arrangements, had killed herself six months later.

The report stated my mother's parents had divorced right after her birth, and her father, an attorney, had been caught in a legal scandal in which he had embezzled money. Her mother had died in 1948 when my mother was twenty, and my mother "recalled the first episode of cutting her wrist and injuring herself occurred shortly after the time of her mother's death." Another chill ran through me as I leaned back and saw the black, dark rainy road and the bridge railing I had nearly gone over in my suicide attempt after finding my mother died by suicide.

On July 6, 1962, my mother's status changed from outpatient to inpatient. She said she was married to an alcoholic bartender (my father, William Francis Ohrstrom) and they fought frequently. "She is also self-destructive in that she has cut her right arm many times with sharp glass or a knife … and sometimes she gets so angry with herself that she will even dig her fingernails into the skin of her legs and scratch herself deeply."

My god. This was my mother! She was so sick. God, god, god. If only someone, anyone could have helped her … This happened a full eight years before she finally killed herself in 1970 … was there no way to prevent a suicide in such an ill person? No way to save my mother? No way she could have been kept alive or kept herself alive so that I could meet her, finally, nine years later?

The note went on, repeating the same sadomasochistic diagnosis as earlier, but justified it by saying she tried to get men to hurt her because she had an intensely ambivalent relationship with her mother. Yeah. Whatever that meant. It was the early sixties after all, before the women's movement, before women had even been studied in terms of the medicines that might treat mental illness—and the medicines were not the medicines we have today anyway. Oh yeah, she should have stopped drinking. She should have. But the picture I saw emerging showed a much more complex set of circumstances that led to her death, some self-inflicted and some not. She must have struggled to withstand the siren call of suicide all those years—a call that came each and every day, in thought, moving image, and sound. She fit the profile of many suicides in that she did seek help, not once, not twice, but many times.

A note dated July 18, 1962, stated "patient went U.A. today. Method of escape: from parole." "Telegram sent to husband. Bureau of Records notified." The summary note said she was ambivalent about treatment, and in a rare sentence demonstrating the frustration the doctor felt about helping her, he wrote: "How in the world we are to defeat her self-defeatism is beyond me. This is the main problem, and I think unless this problem is overcome, she will continue to destroy herself piece by piece."

She was rehospitalized in December 1963 for another suicide attempt, in which she put her head in the lighted gas oven after the birth of Amanda, her seventh and last child. This could be the time about which Karen had told me she and Camille were visiting our mother, and were temporarily placed in foster care after our mother had made a suicide attempt. She stayed in the ward of the hospital until discharged on January 10, 1964. Why didn't the doctors at the hospital keep her there? *They should have kept her there.* I closed my eyes and mouthed the words, my face contorted into a grimace. They should have kept her there.

She was hospitalized again on April 12, 1965, after hearing of her brother Kenneth's death. "She [had also] encountered an example of sadism in the nursing home where she had been working. A fellow employee was abusive and cruel to a helpless old female patient." She had also run out of her medicine, Elavil, and in a sign of the times, the doctor had noted she was "premenstrual." However, despite her record, she was discharged to her job and apartment to continue psychotherapy on the following day, April 13.

In July 1966 the police again arrested her for drunkenness, but the note gave no further information. The records had a bunch of faded, handwritten pages and notes from the staff about her day-to-day progress, but they were illegible or did not have the depth of information contained in the written reports.

So that was it. My legacy from my mother: incomplete mental health records. She was depressed. She was alcoholic. She had a sadomasochistic relationship with men. Psychoneurotic. Passive-aggressive personality. No psychosis, but at one point, a psychotic episode where she thought people were trying to murder her. She had been prescribed Elavil and Antabuse. Doctors had noted how ill she was, they had repeatedly discharged her when it seemed clear she needed long-term care.

She was depressed. Of course, she was depressed. She had given up her oldest three children to her first husband, and her youngest three children had been removed from her care. The woman in these records had suffered greatly. She had tried to stop drinking and succeeded at different times. But she was sick with a disease that still kills people today, a disease that I carry today: depression. What a simple word. What agony, what relentless cruelty suicidal thoughts and gestures have. It is difficult for those who have not experienced the pervasiveness of suicidal thoughts to imagine the hundreds of times these thoughts pass through one's mind, unbidden and uncontrolled, each stinking, lousy day.

It would have been easier to hate my mother, to condemn her for being weak. I just wanted to cry. I didn't hate her. She was my mother. How could I hate someone who became upset at cruelty in a nursing home? How could I hate someone who tried so hard to get help, even if her attempts were "ambivalent"? Her later attempts didn't seem ambivalent to me. Oh, why couldn't the doctors and therapists help her? She was my mother, now she was dead, and no one could change anything.

I hated that she drank; I have always hated alcoholism. But I didn't hate her. In fact, I thought I would have liked her—the woman who wrote about the movie *The Outsiders* and worried her son would get sent away in the draft. The woman who was upset about losing her kids. That woman. She seemed like she loved us despite being incapable of parenting. And now she was dead, and I'd never know what the love of my mother would have felt like. I would never even get mad at her or ask her what happened or see her wear one of her black sheath dresses.

Here I was, grown and educated, sitting in a café in San Francisco, wishing I could see my mother one more time, one more time that I could remember and treasure. Here I was, and a part of me felt like a lost little girl who wanted to throw her arms around her mother's knees and never let go. Here I was, a grown woman, wanting to hold my mother's face, look into her eyes, and tell her she was worth something to me, she had always been worth something to me, and I wished she loved herself the way I loved her.

But the cards didn't fall my way this time, I told myself. The cards didn't fall my way. I rubbed my eyes and pushed back into my chair, suddenly back in the present moment of a café once again. It was time to leave. I carefully rebundled the papers for which I had fought so hard and walked into the gray streets of the city. I walked for a long time.

CHAPTER 5

Back to the Beginning

5 November, 1990

Division of Social Services
Commonwealth of Massachusetts
150 Causeway Street
Boston MA 02114
Attn: Diane Frost

Dear Ms. Frost:

My name is Barbara Ohrstrom. I am thirty years of age. I am writing to you because I would like you and the Division of Social Services to know the effects your decisions back in 1962 through 1965 have had on my life. Too often, decisions are made by agencies such as yours without any knowledge of the final outcome. This is one final outcome I would like you to know about. Perhaps if you had more knowledge about the effects on people's lives Social Services has, better decisions would be made.

I have discovered the general facts of my early life through a lot of research and trouble. My siblings and I came to the attention of your organization in 1962. My mother, Joan Audrey Ohrstrom, was mentally unstable, and had shown she was an incompetent parent. My father, William Francis Ohrstrom, had deserted her, leaving her alone with six small children. My mother's sister sent the three eldest children to live with their natural father, a man named Mr. Joseph, but my twin brother Billy, sister Sue, and myself were put into the care and custody of the Commonwealth of Massachusetts.

On September 14, 1962, two social workers came to my mother's apartment and took the three of us from my mother and placed us in separate foster homes. My brother and I were two years old, and my sister was three. I still have no recollection of this foster home. I do not know who these people were.

I was placed with Gladys Power and her family in December 1962. Gladys believed I was not cared for in the first foster home. Apparently, I was in very poor physical condition when I reached Gladys Power's home. I was covered with a rash, and I had a severe burn covering my back that was infected. Gladys said I did not learn to walk or speak until I was nearly four. Therefore, it appears I was neglected in this first foster home, and I suspect abuse as well, because I am beginning to remember my early childhood.

My twin brother and sister were also placed with Gladys Power and her family in December 1962, and so we were reunited. The Powers loved us and took good care of us. At this home, my brother, sister, and I became healthy and happy young children.

I also learned that either you or another representative of your agency thought I was retarded, and there was talk of placing me in a home for retarded children. Apparently, no one made the obvious connection between my inability to walk or speak and the burn and neglect from the first foster home. Fortunately, that decision to place me in a home for retarded children never materialized, and so two and one half nurturing, loving years passed for the three of us in the Powers' home.

The Powers became very attached to the three of us, and discussed adoption with the Division of Social Services. However, either you or someone else reassured the Powers that "no one would want to adopt three children because three were too many and the children were too old." As insurance, however, someone asked the Powers to sign a waiver, stating that they would never attempt to adopt us. The Powers signed the waiver, trusting that we would grow up in their home.

In 1965, Al and Marie Malfide were approved for adoption. This in itself is astounding, because Al Malfide had been married three times and had already abandoned his own birth son to an alcoholic mother and her parents. I find it amazing the state could not find this out in any kind of a cursory investigation.

At any rate, they wanted two children, but not infants. You or someone else bargained with them. You told them that you had three children and it would be a shame to split them up. Al and Marie agreed, and so the bargain was struck.

On a hot day in June 1965, you came to the Powers' house in a sedan with Al and Marie. We were told to sit in the backseat, and we did. We sat in that backseat without a single possession—not one set of clothes, not one doll, not one memento of the only love we had ever known, from the Powers. You and Al and Marie talked as if we did not exist, and it was evident you were talking about the three of us. I turned around, stared out the back windshield, and saw my foster father hold my foster mother while she cried, and then I knew, and my brother and sister knew, that something terrible had just happened.

Apparently, neither you, Marie, nor Al thought our feelings about our foster parents were important enough to talk about. You didn't think we would understand or know that we were being taken from the only people who had ever cared for us and nurtured us, where we had spent two and a half happy years. I don't know what you thought about, but you cannot tell me you ever thought about the welfare of three small children who had no choices but to sit in the backseat of that car and go into the home of strangers.

You also cut the only link to our birth parents, because both my mother and father visited us and brought us presents while we lived at the Powers. My parents weren't good parents, but they cared enough to come and visit us while we lived with people who were wonderful parents. I never had the chance to know my mother or father because of the adoption, and now I never will, because my birth parents are dead.

Because of the abysmally poor investigation of Al and Marie Malfide, you and the Division of Social Services placed us in an adoptive home that was the equivalent of a concentration camp. My adoptive father was a tyrant, and like all tyrants, he practiced his tyranny where he could—on three parentless children.

I know this letter, whoever reads it, is difficult to read. It's probably taken you maybe five or ten minutes to read this far. And it's pretty uncomfortable. No one likes to know her decisions were not right. My sister, brother, and I have been uncomfortable for a lot longer than five or ten minutes. One instance of being sexually molested lasted longer than five or ten minutes, and there were hundreds of those instances.

Until the Division of Social Services changes its focus, and until it and you find ways to treat children as human beings with feelings and civil rights, DSS will continue to make decisions that shatter people's lives. My family has to live with the decisions of the Division of Social Services for the rest of our lives.

A famous poet wrote, "There is nothing as defenseless as a motherless child." In the case of myself, my brother, and my sister, I think we can shorten that to there is nothing as defenseless as a child. You, in your day-to-day functions, have chosen to uphold a massive responsibility. You are the only people who stand in the way of torture and neglect of thousands and thousands of children. You are needed. People like me needed you to honor and uphold your responsibility every single day. Cutting corners with children means things happen like what happened to my brother, sister, and me. When you cut a corner, you are cutting up a child's soul.

So today, and every day, you go out there into that world, where children are counting on you and depending on you, and you remember that. You remember that child has no defense, no advocate except you. If you fail, a part of that child dies.

Sincerely,

Barbara Ohrstrom

cc: Commissioner Marie Matava

Governor Michael Dukakis

Hon. Edward Kennedy

I received compassionate replies to this letter from Senator Kennedy and Eileen Torpey of the Division of Social Services. My clarion call at the end of my letter inspired DSS to post this letter in their thirty-one field placement offices. It didn't undo the damage, but it proved one of my favorite pieces of life wisdom: when I act to help others, I heal.

BARBARA LEIGH OHRSTROM

MARIE A. MATAVA
COMMISSIONER

150 CAUSEWAY STREET
BOSTON, MA 02114
TEL: (617) 727-0900
FAX: (617) 723-5148

March 7, 1991

Ms. Barbara Ohrstrom
P.O. Box 11318
Oakland, CA 92611-1318

Dear Ms. Ohrstrom:

Your moving and articulate testimony about your adoption
experience has been read by many levels of administrators in this
agency. I have been asked to write to you in response and acknowledge-
ment because of my long history of adoption practice in the public agencies in Massachusets.

Implicit in an adoption plan is the promise to birth parents
that their children would receive better parenting than they themselves
could offer; the promise to foster parents that their love and attach-
ment would be matched and bettered with more assurances of long term
commitment; the promise to children of a "forever" family in which to
grow up in love, continuity, safety and emotional health. For you and
your loved ones none of these promises were met and for this we are
heartily sorry.

Over the past twenty five years we have learned much about
adoption, usually from hearing from families and individuals like yourself. We now focus on our first responsibility which is to preserve
biological families by offering parents the help they need to adequately parent their children. No child can be considered for adoption
planning unless our agency demonstrates to an impartial review board, as
well as to the Probate Courts of Massachusetts that intensive services
have been offered to biological families for a least one year, often
much longer, in order for them to achieve that rehabilitation necessary
to have their children retruned to their care. The majority of families
involved with our agency in these past few years do have their children
returned to them, since with appropriate help they were able to overcome
the problems which adversely affected their parenting.

When children cannot return home and adoption becomes the plan
of choice, a child's current foster parent, by state law and agency
policy, is given first consideration as the adoptive parent. In fact
currently in Massachusetts approximately 75% of the average 500 children
adopted each year are adopted by their foster parents. This practice is
obviously a far cry from the practice of the 1960's when foster parents
were not "allowed" to adopt children in their care.

All adoptive parents, as well as all foster parents, since 1984, must participate in a thirty hour, ten week, educational/assessment program before they can be considered to have a child placed with them. During this Family Resource Program there are very telling issues discussed and families are being observed over time, and then individually evaluated. Social workers are better able to assess applicants' overall personality, their marital relationship, and their responses to some of the very relevant materials presented. We certainly get to know these families in a much more comprehensive way than in past years.

Decisions about placing particular children in particular homes are made by a multidisciplinary team. When foster parents are not interested in adopting a particular child in their home, the foster parents who know the child best can be an integral part of the team which attempts to best "match" the needs of a child with the strengths of a potential adoptive family.

Moving children from one family to another has been described as more intricate than transplanting a heart from one human being to another. We have learned that adequately preparing a child for adoption is imperative. Social workers and mental health therapists work with children over time in order to help them understand why they cannot return to their biological families, and to involve them in planning for their adoption. Each child with their social worker, develops a life story book in which both the positive, as well as the painful, events of their lives are explored and explained.

Children are no longer "placed for adoption" without a prolonged pre-placement period. Children meet prospective adoptive families, visit them first for short visits, moving to day visits, increasing to over night visits, then to more prolonged weekend or weeklong visits. During this "pre-placement" period the adoption worker and the foster parent, as well as the child's therapist, assess the appropriateness of the family resoruce. They give the child clear messages that their feelings and observations about the family can be shared in safety. After placement, most families are expected to have the children involved with a mental health therapist. In the year before the adoption is legalized, the agency social worker makes frequent visits to collaborate with schools, therapists, and other outside caregivers, as well as, the family and the children directly to assess the appropriateness of the placement.

-3-

I came to the Department of Public Welfare as a new adoption worker in 1968. I have seen first hand all these changes, but I have also seen the pain that accompanied this progress in developing a better understanding of the adoption process. We who have read your letter are impressed not only by your incredible inner strength, but also the aura of warmth and human concern that laces the text of your letter. Thank you for sharing this painful information and your feelings with us. As you permit, I have made a copy of your letter and sent it to the thirty one adoption supervisors and their administrators who are today responsible for making adoption plans for children in the care of this "child welfare" agency. It is important for us, on a daily basis, to tune our conscience to the tremendous impact our decision making has on so many peoples lives and the ethical implications of implementing that authority. Thank you for the courage of your convictions.

Sincerely,

Eileen E. Torpey
Statewide Adoption Services Coordinator

EET/mk

Thus far, I had obtained my adoption records, my mother's psychiatric records, and various bits of the story from my sisters and brother, Karen, Camille, and Kevin, and my foster mother Gladys. Only one set of records I had not seen remained: mine from the Division of Social Services.

What did I know? I knew my parents had not consented to the adoption, a fact that still made me feel less unwanted. My mother's signature had been annexed because she had suffered institutionalization, and my father's whereabouts had been listed as unknown. According to my newly found siblings, my older sisters Sue and Camille, at the time two and three years old, had left me in the tub with the hot water running, burning me and leaving me with a scar I carry to this day. Someone from the Division of Social Services had placed my sister Sue, my twin Bill, and me in separate foster care homes on September 14, 1962. Then, in December 1962, we had been moved again, to the home of Gladys and Bill Power. Finally, in June 1965, Marie and Al took us and subsequently adopted us. Now I wanted to find some of the details that would lend color to the starkness of these few facts.

JANUARY 30, 1992
MILL VALLEY, CA

I wrote a letter to Eileen Torpey, adoption supervisor, with whom I had corresponded in the past, asking for the release of my Division of Social Services records. She mailed them to me; it was that easy. I didn't know from what basement, crate, or building they had dug up those records, but I was amazed the records had remained intact and available after all these years. I sat in yet another café, reading another set of records, trying to sift through the information and match it with what I already knew.

This time, I felt the pain as soon as I started to read; the social worker who had kept these records probably never imagined the subject of them would one day, finally, read them.

FEBRUARY 19, 1992
24 FARNSWORTH STREET
BOSTON, MA 02210

Dear Barbara,

Please find enclosed the information on yourself and your biological parents that is contained in the agency adoption record, which speaks to your earliest foster care experiences and the nature of termination of parental rights.

There should be visit-to-visit summary dictation of the social worker's contacts with your birth parents, which I am in the process of trying to locate. A copy of such should have been in your adoption record but was not, so I am skeptical I will be able to find it, but I am trying.

As you will notice, your birth mother voluntarily surrendered you three children for adoption within extenuating [sic] circumstances. The agency requested the court to terminate your birth father's rights as he

131

had failed to continue to work with the agency to plan for you. Please be advised that the statement, "Received under Section 23A" means that the parent, or parents, voluntarily came to the agency requesting foster care placement for their children. According to the record, the agency never took custody from your parents between the time you were placed in foster care and your mother's signing adoption surrenders and the court terminating your father's right to notice of adoption.

I hope this information is helpful to you. Should I find more information (which would be within the next two weeks or so), I will forward it to you.

Sincerely,
Eileen Torpey
Adoption Specialist

My parents, then, had not had DSS workers swarm into our home and forcibly remove us from their care because they were such bad parents. That relieved me: voluntarily surrendering us indicated a caring for our welfare. My parents may not have been good parents, but neither were they uncaring brutes.

I sat down and started reading through the records filled with notes by state caseworkers, quoted below.

9/14/62 (F.N., the initials of our caseworker.) Mr. Ohrstrom brought the three children to the office for placement, as we had arranged previously.... Mr. Ohrstrom accompanied me in placing the children and spoke of his concern for them and for his wife. He said that when she was not drinking, she took very good care of the children and was a good mother to them. He admits that he drinks himself and frequently loses his temper with his wife. The children played in the backseat on the trip to Mendon. They were dirty, and it was evident that they had not received much care in recent days.... Mr. Ohrstrom and the children cried as we left....

This happened at the time my mother went into the psychiatric hospital, and it was my father who had surrendered us for foster care placement— but not for adoption. Oh and that last line: sometimes even records show the human cost of all of this foster placement.

9/19/62 (F. N.) The foster mother feels that there is something wrong with Barbara. She stays in any position she is put in and does not move herself until she is moved by someone. She seems to have some mongoloid features.

That retarded issue again. Hadn't Gladys said something about that? Why did they think I was retarded?

10/15/62 (F. N.) Letter received from foster mother that she is having a difficult time with the children. None of them are trained, and she has found them quite a handful. Mr. Ohrstrom has been visiting weekly, despite the fact that this has been discussed with both him and the foster mother and arrangements were made for visits every other week.

I smiled. My father was persistent in his visits. At the same time, I wanted to cry: the fact my brother, sister, and I were untrained and quite a handful told me we were not taken care of by my mother as well as my father may have wanted to think we were.

10/19/62 (F. N.) Foster mother is finding herself overwhelmed caring for these three children, together with her own three and the other foster child in her home. Billy and Barbara are not trained, and Susan has frequent accidents.... Foster mother feels the children are responding well. Barbara walks all the time now. She doesn't speak, but she does seem more alert than at the time she was placed. Mr. Ohrstrom visits the children weekly.... They remember him from week to week and seem very happy to see him. He calls during the week to see how they are and brings them a small gift each time he comes. Foster mother does not feel she can care for the three children much longer.

Once again, I am surprised by my father's caring and persistence. He certainly broke the stereotype about the young father who gets the young mother pregnant and then disappears.

10/23/62 (F. N.) Today I called another foster parent in Mendon concerning placement of Susan with her.... Foster parent called later to say that new foster parent will pick up Susan this afternoon.

The flatness of the statement showed nothing of the shock this must have caused for the three of us at that time. I had not remembered my sister had been separated from Bill and me. How traumatizing that must have been for all three of us. What if that separation had been permanent? Did it scar my sister? It must have. All throughout our childhoods, we three had operated like a unit—inseparable. Despite differences my sister and I have had, I knew she had protected me and would fight for me, as I would and had for her at any given point in time. Bill, Sue, and I were mother, father, aunt, uncle, cousin, and grandparents to one another. We had made pacts when we were children recognizing this fact: we were alone, and we would always stand for and by one another. I couldn't imagine any minute of my life without my sister ... and to think I had lost her on October 23, 1962, and not even known she was gone.

10/29/62 (F. N.) Today Mrs. Ohrstrom came to the office. She said that Barbara's general health had been good. Barbara has not had any DPT or polio inoculations and had not walked until her placement in the first foster home. Mrs. Ohrstrom had felt Barbara might be retarded. She brought her to City Hospital in Worcester for different tests, which she claims were negative.

The hospital records were also enclosed, and I jumped ahead and riffled through them. Just as my mother had said, the tests were negative. But how could my mother say my general health had been good when that burn had occurred? Maybe it was healed by then. But didn't social workers know that a burn of that magnitude (I can still feel the lumps of scar tissue in my back) would have had an effect on development? This retarded issue certainly would not go away.

12/17/62 (F. N.) Mrs. Gladys Power was contacted and asked if she would be willing to take the three Ohrstrom children.

12/21/62 (F. N.) Children were moved to the home of Mrs. Gladys Power, West Boylston. Mr. Ohrstrom called requesting permission to visit on 12/24/62. Permission was granted.

I sighed in relief. That was how it came to pass that we were all reunited and placed together: Mrs. Power had agreed to take the three of us. Her generosity and decency reunited us. It seemed the choices of adults changed our fate as the breezes move leaves first one way, then another. What if she had said no? What if Mrs. Power had wanted only one child instead of "the twins"? What a debt the three of us owed Gladys, who, over the course of a telephone call, preserved the family unit of three small children whom she had never met or known.

12/27/62 (E. J. C., initials of a new caseworker.) Foster mother had taken Barbara to the doctor to have the infection checked. The infection appears to have cleared up.

4/2/63 (E. J. C.) Barbara's adjustment to the Powers' foster home has been extremely good. Definite improvement has been seen in her ability to respond to the affection of the foster parents. Barbara shows no fear of the family unit. Foster mother told Worker that Barbara seeks attention in various ways—for example: she insists upon kissing all members of the foster family "good night," meeting foster mother's children when they come home from school, and always attempting to follow foster father wherever he may be going. She has not had the rash she had in the first foster home. She is much more friendly and talkative than she was previously. Foster mother told me she is now toilet trained.

Perhaps the happiness—or perhaps the loss—inherent in this paragraph made tears well in my eyes.

9/19/ & 10/31/63 (E. J. C.) Of the three Ohrstrom children placed in the Powers' foster home, Barbara is the one who has benefited the most.... She is affectionate toward all members of the family and seems to display a close bond with both her sister and twin brother.

12/4/63 (*E. J. B. Initials of same caseworker who apparently had gotten married.*) Barbara's adjustment in the foster home continues to be outstanding. She has come a long way in her development and shows no signs of retardation, which had been questioned previously. She readily responds to the affections of the foster family and, according to Mrs. Power, her surroundings. She seems to be more adventurous and more independent than either of her siblings, hence, more mischievous. She is walking better than she was previously but still does not like to wear shoes. Foster mother says Barbara will keep her shoes on for an hour or so, then off they come. She has checked to make sure the shoes fit well, which they do, but still Barbara refuses to keep them on. She plays well, both alone and with her siblings.

I smiled despite my tears; I still hate shoes and take them off the first chance I get.

Summary of Visits: 3/1964, 4/28/64, 6/30/64, 8/18/64, & 10/6/64 (J. L. E.) On every visit, Barbara has immediately recognized Worker and always runs to the car to welcome her. Foster mother reports that Barbara plays very well with the other children and seems to be making terrific progress in development and learning. She now knows all the letters and all the numbers and points them out on signs along the road, in magazines, etc. Barbara is quite possessive of foster mother and doesn't want her to go anywhere without her. The first week that her sister, Susan, went to school, Barbara cried every day because she wanted to get on the bus and go to school also. Now that she is used to Susan going to school every day, it does not bother her.

Probably fearful of losing people I loved, it doesn't surprise me I was possessive of Gladys and cried when Sue left for kindergarten, given that I had been separated from my mother and temporarily separated from Sue.

Summary of Visits from November 1964 to June 1965 (J. L. E.) Barbara continues to be very friendly when Worker visits and always runs to the car or the door of the house to welcome Worker when she arrives. During late winter and early spring, Barbara began going through the negative stage that her twin brother, Billy, went through six months before. Whereas Billy has learned to write his name and write the letters of the alphabet, Barbara has no interest whatsoever in anything to do with writing. She plays well with the other children and is eagerly looking forward to going to kindergarten next year. In June, Barbara began to take an interest in learning to write, again six months later than Billy. However, Barbara is left-handed and is presently writing and reading backward. Not only are her letters backward, but she writes from right to left instead of left to right. Foster mother has discussed this with school and has been assured that this often happens with left-handed children and they eventually grow out of it.

The notes ended there. Why did the social workers take us away from such a happy home, a home in which they themselves thought Sue, Billy, and I were doing well?

MASSACHUSETTS DEPARTMENT OF PUBLIC WELFARE

TO:
John R. M., Director DCG Date: Oct. 1, 1963
(John J. S., Attorney, DCG)

FROM:
Ethyl J. M., District Director, Worcester
James F. M., Child Welfare Supervisor

RE:
Susan Ohrstrom, born 7/27/59 – DCG 54099-A
Barbara Ohrstrom, born 8/6/60 – DCG 54099-B
William Ohrstrom, born 8/6/60 – DCG 54099-C

We are requesting action under Chapter 210, Section 3A on the behalf of the above named children received into the care of the Division of Child Guardianship on 9/12/62 under section 23A.

Father: William Francis Ohrstrom, born 4/2/30. First marriage, date unknown; divorce obtained 6/15/53. Second marriage 3/3/60 to Joan Audrey (Morris) (C.) Ohrstrom. Occupation: Bartender. Last known address is 123 Dean Street, Worcester.

Mother: Joan Audrey (Morris) (C.) Ohrstrom, born 4/2/30 [s/b 10/17/27]. First marriage to Mr. Joseph, date unknown. There were three children by this marriage, custody of whom was granted to Mr. Joseph when the divorce was granted. Second marriage to William Ohrstrom on 3/3/60. Three children resulted from this marriage—the three for whom this petition is being filed.

William, Barbara, and Susan Ohrstrom were taken into the care of the Division of Child Guardianship under Section 23A signed by their father on 9/14/62. Intensive work was started with both parents to make plans for the future of the three children. Mrs. Ohrstrom, who had been a patient at Worcester State Hospital from 7/6/62 to 7/25/62 (diagnosis of alcoholism with psychoneurotic depression), returned to State Hospital on an outpatient basis. She desired to obtain a divorce from her husband because of his drinking problem and brutality. Both parents came to the office on a weekly basis and freely discussed their problems. Mr. Ohrstrom finally agreed to the divorce. He encouraged his wife to make plans for the children. She acquired a furnished apartment and plans were established to return Susan home first, and with close supervision she would work toward eventually acquiring the other two children. The day before Susan was to go with her mother, she called and said she had received a visit from her first husband, Mr. Joseph and that he desired that she take the two oldest children of her first marriage. She said that Mr. Ohrstrom knew nothing about this. His visits to the office had become less frequent. Mrs. Ohrstrom, realizing that she could not care for five children, made the decision to release the three children by her second marriage for adoption. She signed the releases on June 17, 1963.

Mr. Ohrstrom was contacted and told of his wife's decision. He refused to release the children for adoption, saying that he was going to make plans for them. He planned to get a housekeeper and make a home for them. He was supported in this and told that we would fully cooperate; however, that he must do something soon. In the past three months, he has not been heard from nor has he made any effort to contact the children. Efforts have been made to contact him; however, he has not responded. He realizes what Chapter 210 is as it was fully explained, and he is aware that we planned to use this action if he did not make an effort to provide for these children. This man's emotional maturity is so nominal that his plans have the essence of dreams. His heavy drinking coupled with his immaturity leaves little hope that his situation will improve. The three children have been damaged already; however, after a year of good foster care, they are bright, normal little children who would easily be adopted.

The plans for our adoption had begun in 1963, two full years before Marie and Al came and took us from the Powers. I stopped reading and shut my eyes when I read the line about my mother. So she *had* signed us away. I could only imagine the turmoil and pain this decision cost her. She had two choices: sign the papers or take us back. It was clear from the memorandum she felt incapable of providing a home for the three of us. If I could tell her anything, if I could have just one hour with her, I would tell her how sorry I was events transpired in this way. I would tell her I knew she was desperately ill with a disease doctors didn't have the tools to treat in 1963. I understood she thought she made the best decision for us; she never dreamed we would be placed in the adoptive home in which we were—she could not have predicted that. She must have thought we'd be placed in a home with parents who could care for us, dream for us, and build for us the lives she knew she couldn't give us.

My father disappeared. His attempts to take care of us moved me. Despite his fantasies and inability to cope, it was clear he, too, had cared about us, loved us, wanted what was best for us. It must have felt shameful and excruciating to realize he could not handle the responsibility of caring for his three children, whom he had so diligently visited in the foster homes for a short period of time. He tried, however ineptly, to give us a home.

The memo had an air of inevitability about it; it was inevitable we get adopted. DCG, it appeared, had pressured my parents to take responsibility for us or sign us away; it didn't seem a middle ground existed in which we could have stayed with the Powers forever and our parents could have visited us. "Easily be adopted." I shook my head. It made us sound like commodities: flour or sugar or beets.

At last, I knew the truth; I knew everything. My parents were neither heroes, victims, nor villains, but troubled and problematic people incapable of providing for their children despite their best wishes. DCG had made a terrible mistake in the adoption, even though they seemed staffed by people of good intent who followed policy. I suspect the happy middle ground I had staked out did not exist; that is, DCG may have faced legislative pressure through their funding to clear their rolls. After all, adoptive parents do not take payments each month from the state of Massachusetts, a.k.a. the good taxpayers of the state.

But oh! The human cost of this tragedy is incalculable. Once blame was removed, once villainy was not ascribed, then the pain of that decision swept through me like a hurricane. If we were damaged from the move to the first foster home, and then to the Powers' home, how much more damaged were we by the move to Al and Marie's home? And to couple that move, that damage alone, with the abuse Marie and Al inflicted? It seemed the system itself was incapable of calculating the human suffering its decisions, policies, and movements caused.

Furthermore, how much pain had the Powers endured by losing us when we had been part of their family? Perhaps receiving these records helped to pave the way for the reunion that eventually took place between the only woman who treated me as her daughter, my foster mother, Gladys Power. I had been busily writing to Gladys Power and slowly telling her about who I was and what had happened.

MARCH 1990
SAN FRANCISCO, CA

My foster mother, Gladys Power, and I had sent polite Christmas cards back and forth for ten years until 1989. I had sent her a card that year but didn't hear from her until February, when she wrote me a short note, and so I decided to write her a letter.

MARCH 29, 1990
PO Box 11318
OAKLAND, CA 94611-1318

Dear Gladys,

This is the second or third letter I've started to you—there's so much to tell you I don't know where to begin—maybe at the end and work backward.

I've got a job as a legal secretary; although it pays the bills (especially those student loans), I'm not happy—because I'm out of my field. I am applying for teaching jobs at several community colleges in the area, and I think one of them will come through with a teaching position. I taught at Emerson College for two years while I was getting my MA there.

I live in a nice neighborhood in SF, close to Bill's house (he lives right down the hill). He is doing well—he also works at a law firm doing their billing, and he is still painting and trying to make his way as an artist. We have dinner once a week or so, and our relationship has evolved into being real pals. We can count on each other. He's as humorous and smart-alecky as ever—some things never change!

I moved out here in the beginning of 1989 to give Bill some support because he was going through tough times. Things are better now, and I think it's been good for me to be out here too. I miss New England fiercely, and someday I hope to come back … however, it's nice living close to Bill because we were separated for a long time. He's been living out here for five years.

I wrote a book about adoption and am now in the slow and tedious process of rewriting it. I hope to publish it in a couple more years. It's slow going with these kinds of projects, so time will tell.

I also started a support group for women who were adopted. We all have different stories, and some of us made out better than others; some of us searched and found bad news, and some of us didn't search, and some of us are in the process of it. It's hard to believe ten years have gone by since we reunited in '79; I was so shy and afraid of infringing on you or of bringing up bad memories, I let a wonderful chance to know you slip away. I'm glad you wrote to me way back then, and I still have your letter, and I'm glad you wrote to me now.

I don't know how much Sue and I knew when we had dinner with you or how much we were able to tell you—we were both young, afraid, and shy, and probably not open, although we wanted to be. There's so much I want to thank you and your family for. Your generosity back in

1962 probably saved my life. Not only that; although my memories of staying with you are poor, I remember feeling a lot of love and laughter and healing—and although I was too young to appreciate what you did then and don't remember enough to fully thank you now, I believe that you and your family were a godsend to Billy, Sue, and me, and I can never thank you enough for that. The stay we had in your home was the happiest part of my childhood. Although I don't know what it was like for you to take care of two infants and a three-year-old—and one of those infants with a life-threatening burn, I can imagine how it must have been. (I still have the scar from that burn today, and I found out years later that Sue and Camille put me in a tub and turned the hot water on—they were only little kids and didn't know what they were doing.)

I think Sue and I told you this, but in case you didn't know, I found out our mother died in 1970, and our father died in 1980. That was disappointing and painful for me (and still is, sometimes). It's hard for other people to understand, because they see adoption as something that wipes out a person's past, but it doesn't. It seems my mother was a troubled woman, but it seems she really loved all of us but just couldn't manage to carry the load—I suspect that's something you may know more about than others.

I remember clearly the day we went to live with the Malfides. I remember looking out the back window and seeing you and our foster father standing on the lawn looking sad, and we didn't understand what was happening to us. We had a hard time adjusting to losing you and your family and, most of all, your love.

I guess I knew all along I would want to write about this stuff to you—I hope it's okay. It's all had so much to do with who I am now and why I believe the things I do, and I am so lucky you are here and willing to correspond with me.

I know my adoptive mother Marie had written a letter in "Confidential Chat" (similar to Dear Abby" and you had answered it; I believe the two of you wrote back and forth for a while. It's so criminal and insensitive that the Department of Social Services didn't have more sensitivity to the feelings of everyone involved—it was so wrong none of us could stay in touch with one another. And then, it was hard to stay in touch because things were so painful and I didn't know how to face that, and I didn't know how to nor could I tell you how things really happened.

Anyway, from the great vantage point of nearly thirty, and having read a lot of books and gone to counseling for a while and talked with other people, I understand myself better now and have come to terms with some things. (*Atlantic* magazine just ran a front-page, fairly dry and scientific article on separation and children and basically concluded separation was not a good thing—they just had to ask me, I could have told them!) I have always had tremendous fears of abandonment and have a hard time getting close to other people as a result—and it is something that has stopped me from having children myself, although I love children, because I am terrified they would get taken away from me somehow or I would get killed and what would happen to them? I have also always been afraid of fires and had an irrational fear of stepping into a tub—just a hesitancy, really—and never took baths—always showers, and no wonder, because of that burn. Things hang around and affect you years after things happen.

I found out six of us children had been in a fire in Worcester, and my older brother (Kevin) and sister (Karen) pulled us out of it. I remember nothing of this—it's as if my life is still a puzzle and gradually, through bits and pieces of offhand remarks and stories from different people, I have been able to piece together the events from back then. I know we were in foster homes before coming to live with you, but I have no idea where or with whom—although I suspect it must not have been a good situation because that burn was in such poor condition when I came to live with you.

Living with the Malfides was also difficult. My adoptive mother loved us, but she was not prepared to deal with us that well, and that probably would have been okay, but Al, our adoptive father, was an extremely violent man once behind closed doors and so—things were rather difficult.

All those things notwithstanding, Billy, Sue, and I have evolved into fairly healthy and caring adults. Our parents must have been intelligent, seeing we ended up with a good amount of brains. (Although from my grammar in this letter, you'd never know it!) Your portrayal of Bill as being a "mischievous fellow" hit the nail on the head! Sue is the more retiring of the three of us. Her shyness has often been mistaken for arrogance or aloofness, but she is neither. She is sensitive and easily hurt, and tries hard to succeed in all her endeavors. She earned a BA from Northeastern in Criminal Justice and is working at an insurance firm processing workers' comp claims—which, I gather, can be complicated and involves legalese and bureaucratic hoops. As for me—I am the sentimental one of the three, and aware of my feelings about things. The smallest gesture of kindness from anyone always moves me because I know the kindness of people such as you are to what I owe my life.

Billy and I were both in a home for troubled teens many years ago, and people there were good to both of us. Sue and I put ourselves through college and had positive experiences there. I was active on the school paper and magazine and wrote a lot about human rights issues. I hope to eventually get myself in a position where I can speak for kids in the same situation we were in and try to reform the social services systems in the nation so things are done in a less haphazard way. I think getting my book published is a big step in the right direction—and of course, I love teaching, because it allows me to talk to teenagers about what is going on in their lives. It's a way for me to turn a difficult experience into something that gives understanding to others. I read in a book [Victor Frankl's Man's Search for Meaning] that suffering has no meaning other than the meaning one gives it, and I believe in that.

Sue and I are avid readers and can put away a book a day when we feel like it. I just finished yet another book by James Baldwin yesterday and am reading Joyce Carol Oates today. When Sue and I were kids, we would borrow six books from the library, read our own, and then each other's books every single week. I read the entire *Reader's Digest Condensed Books* collection, along with *Sherlock Holmes*, *The Count of Monte Cristo*, *The Three Musketeers*, and countless others. By the time I was a freshman in high school, I was reading at a level of a freshman in college—much to the surprise of the teachers whose classes I was busily flunking. Books have given me understanding—and best of all, an idea of what my possibilities were and wondrous imaginative journeys ... I cannot imagine a world without books.

I've rambled on in an unedited fashion for quite a while here—please forgive the fact this letter is fairly disorganized. There's so much, so many little details to tell—and I let my heart run away with the writing of this letter.

I was wondering if you had any pictures of us. If you would care to write and tell me more about what it was like having us, that would be wonderful. I look forward to hearing from you, and I will write again soon and tell you more about what happened and what is happening. Please tell me how your kids are and how your job is (are you still working?) and what you do now and just anything and everything you want.

Again, thank you so much for everything.

Sincerely,

Barbara Ohrstrom

Two months later, I received a letter from Gladys. It's funny, thinking about it, but she has always used the same stationery and cards on which to write me. The envelopes and paper have roses entwined across the

146

top. I was always happy to hear from her, maybe too happy. After all, I hadn't seen her but once since I was four years old.

MAY 30
WEST BOYLSTON, MA

Dear Barbara,

Like you, I've started this letter a dozen times. We were all glad to get your letter and have all had our little say about what is important to us about your time with us and your leaving.

I guess the one thing we all want to make you understand (Bill and Susan too) is how devastating it was when the state decided you were going to be adopted. An important part of our life was just taken away. As we look back, I realize we all should have had some sort of counseling or therapy. Our family just fell apart, and from 1965–69 were pretty terrible years for us. Of course, it helped when the letter in the *Globe* was printed and I heard from [your adoptive mother]. At least we knew where you were and could stop looking at every child or group of children hoping to see you.

My mother, who now is eighty-seven years old, sends these pictures to you. They were taken sitting on her front steps. Even though she had sixteen grandchildren, she always counted you three and told everyone she and my father had nineteen.

I know the stock answer is, "Well, you knew they were foster children and could be adopted," but after two and a half years, we had become complacent; our social worker assured us no one would ever adopt three children of your ages. And we had signed papers saying we would never try to adopt.

One of the hardest things was answering people's questions, sort of like when someone dies and you keep wishing you could have done something to help them.

This letter is a real downer and I don't mean it to be, but all we want you to know is how much you were loved and what joy you brought to us. We had lots of fun and good times … not a lot of money and material things, but six children in a house made for lots of interesting times.

I am going to write again and try to tell you about your time with us, and I hope you will write again.

Love,

Gladys

I could sense the suffering her family had gone through from her direct and unadorned words. It hit me with the sharpness of a blow. So much suffering, and for what? For getting three children off the foster care rolls, that is, the state payment rolls? For clearing a bureaucratic case? Why had no one seen the suffering, not only of three tiny children, but of the entire Power family? Why had no one responded to the reality of a family torn to shreds, rather than the labels of foster versus adoptive? Why had no one thought the three of us had experienced enough separations and homes and one more switch would hurt us? Most importantly, why had no social workers followed up on the treatment we received from Marie and Al? Decades later, these questions haunt me. However, no answer would ease the hurt of all these injured people.

Gladys and I corresponded for two more years, but in 1991, I did not receive a Christmas card from her. Still too shy to call, I waited, wondering.

FEBRUARY 19, 1992
WEST BOYLSTON, MA

Dear Barbara,

I'm sorry it's been such a long time since I've written, but Bill was very sick and I really didn't have time or inclination to write. He died last Thursday, and we had a memorial service on Sunday. He would have loved it; the church was full, and fifty people came back here. He loved it when we had a crowd here.

I now have to get back into doing things again, and I already have. Yesterday I booked a trip with Elderhostel for the San Francisco Arts and Humanities Center. I'm going to be there from March 27 to April 3, and I certainly hope we'll be able to get together.

I hate to fly, but I have to get away from here for a while.

I'll write more after my plans are final. Please be assured even though I didn't write, I thought of you often.

Love,

Gladys

Tears started in my eyes unexpectedly; I couldn't get her out of my mind. What should I do? A card seemed too casual. A phone call seemed too invasive—what if she didn't want to talk to me? I finally settled on sending flowers, a spring bouquet, four days after I received the letter.

Three days after that, she called. Her voice sounded strong, reassuring, and oddly familiar. She thanked me for the flowers, and I stuttered in reply. Then she told me she was coming to San Francisco and wanted to see me. I stuttered some, and finally told her I couldn't wait to see her. Then she thanked me for the flowers again.

I marked the calendar and began counting the days until she arrived. Every single day, I thought about her. I sent her a short note and told her I was counting the days. I obsessed. Where would we talk? Where could I take her that she would enjoy? Where would we have privacy? What if she didn't want to talk about the past, about what it had been like for us to leave her home?

Finally, Friday, March 27, arrived. I raced home from work and pounced on the telephone when it rang fifteen minutes later. It was Gladys. We agreed I would meet her at the Sheehan Hotel, 620 Sutter Street, in San Francisco the next morning at nine.

I arrived half an hour early and waited in the lobby for fifteen minutes, but unable to wait any longer, I went to her room and tapped on the door.

She opened the door immediately, as if she had been standing there waiting for me. She invited me in. The room was tiny, just a little bed and washstand and dresser. She sat on the bed, and invited me to sit next to her. She put her legs up and looked at me. "Oh, you really do look just like your mother," she said. "Now tell me all about yourself."

I began to cry, and then she began to cry, and then we hugged each other.

I told her a little bit about what I was doing now, and then she began telling me about her grandchildren and children and marriage, and then she told me what it had been like for our family after we were taken away by social workers.

"Bill drank every night after you kids were taken away," she said. "Barbara Gay and Patti moved out. In fact, the day after, Bill decided we should take a trip to Canada to try to forget it all. Well, Patti, Barbara, and Dana fought in the back of the car all the way to the Canadian border. Then we decided we'd had it, and we turned around and drove straight home.

"It was bad for about four or five years. I told Bill he had to stop drinking or I'd divorce him. That snapped him out of it, but honestly, I don't think he was ever the same after you kids were taken." She paused. "None of us were."

"My sister Grace and I used to ride around looking for you kids on the street; it was worse than if you had died because we didn't know where you were."

Gladys waved her hands and wiped her eyes under her glasses. "I told myself I wasn't going to cry, and here I am," she said.

I wiped my eyes too. "You don't know what it's like for me to talk about this. There's so many other people I found, and they don't want to talk about it; they don't want anything to do with me, because it's too painful, all this stuff.

"I remember, right after we got adopted, we went shopping, and I got lost. A saleslady found me. And I asked her, 'Are you my new mommy now?'

"I wish I remembered more about living with you, but I don't. I remember taking a bath upstairs with bubble bath. I remember going grocery shopping and riding in the front of the car." I paused. "I remember being happy."

Gladys smiled when I said that. "You kids came to us right before Christmas. The social worker called me and said you'd only be with us a few days, that they just wanted you together for the holidays so your parents could see you."

"My parents?"

"Oh yes, they came. They brought armloads and armloads of presents for you kids—and we had been worried there wouldn't be enough."

"What were they like?"

"Your sister was close to your father, and she cried when he left. But you and Billy didn't seem too interested in them. But you have to understand, Barbara; you were hurt pretty badly." She paused, and I moved a little closer.

"Those stupid social workers," Gladys said. "They were so callous, so cold. They just brought you kids, said you were retarded, and walked out the door. You were wearing a red snowsuit—I can still see it. The social worker had put you under the tree, and she told me, 'Well, she won't move unless you move her. She may be retarded.' So after she

151

left, I picked you up and took off the snowsuit. You were covered with sores, and they were filled with pus. And when I took off your shoes, your feet were crushed. No wonder you didn't move—it probably hurt too much to move!

"You started coming around pretty fast, although not that night. Of course, I panicked when I saw the sores and ran upstairs and called our family doctor; he was a decent man, lived right up the street. Well, he told me not to worry and to put some ointment on and dress you in loose, comfortable clothes. He said it might be from stress, you know, these sores.

"I remember the first time you walked, how happy we were. The whole family was so excited when you tried to go up the stairs the first time. You used to follow me all over the house.

"Your brother, the first thing he did was grab a Christmas ball and chase the dog. He and Dana got along really well." She laughed. "Oh, he was a character, even then. I remember once Patti brought him to the restaurant where I worked at the time, catering weddings and things like that, and it was a big place, too. Well anyway, Patti brought Billy there, and he ran into the place, ran through the kitchen, and ran into the dining area yelling, 'Mommy, Mommy, I'm here!' Oh, we laughed so hard. He's a character all right. One time I sent him upstairs—he'd been into something, I can't remember what. And he sat at the top of those stairs hollering and carrying on. Then it got quiet, and then, all of a sudden, he says, 'Hey, somebody's yelling up here!'"

I started laughing. "He's still like that," I said.

"And, you, well, I always felt very close to you. You were, you know, like a little wounded bird." She touched my forearm, and went on. "You used to run up to everybody in the house and give them little birdy kisses.

"Susan was the little mother, always watching out for you two. I remember, right after you came, I went up to tuck her in, and I found little pieces of bread under her pillow. And I went downstairs and I said to Bill, 'These kids must have been left hungry; Susan's hiding food upstairs.'

"And all you kids, you were so good. You didn't cry or carry on about anything, and that's not normal for small children. So we knew something bad had happened, but we never found out what it was."

"Well," I said, "my parents took that to their graves."

"I never found how you found us, what happened. I thought Susan found out everything."

"Oh no, it was me," I said. "It's a long, long story." I paused. "I'll tell you one thing, though. As far as I'm concerned," and I looked right at her and took her hand, "you're the only mother I've ever had."

She wiped her eyes again and looked away. "I don't know," she said, "about past lives or anything—oh listen to me, my friends in West Boylston would faint if they heard this—but anyway, well, I feel as if you are mine, you are my daughter, and who knows, maybe we knew each other before …

"I feel as if something that's been hurting for twenty-five years is finished now. I hope we can both go on."

"It's like, uh, it's like everything that happened is undone," I said.

"No, Barbara," she said, "nothing will ever change what happened to you or me or any of us; we can't undo it. But if you want, we can go on; we can come together again as a family and have that now."

I cried a little more, and we held each other's hands and then we hugged.

Gladys reached out and pulled out a tissue and handed it to me. "Well, what do you say?" she said. "How about we go get some breakfast?"

At the restaurant, I noticed we both ordered the same meal: two eggs over easy, bacon, home fries, and whole wheat toast. As I reached to pour cream into my coffee, she smiled and pulled back her hand—she took cream as well.

We took the cable cars to Fisherman's Wharf and walked around. When she saw the boats, she told me, "Bill and I had a boat. He would love to be here with me." She paused, and we both leaned over the rail. "He never read your letters, Barbara. I asked him if he wanted to, and he would say yes, and I would leave them out for him to see. But I think it was too much for him; I think he just couldn't face that a father would do what your adoptive father did to you. You know, there'd be a television special about that on, and he would say, 'I can't believe this really happens; I just can't believe it.'" She looked off into the distance. "But I think he did believe it, and he just couldn't handle it, that it had happened to you.

"I'll never forget the night your sister called. I think it was Thanksgiving or something, and she called to wish us a Happy Thanksgiving. And I said to her, 'Well, are you going home for Thanksgiving?' She said yes. And I said, 'Is Barbara going home with you?' And she started to cry and said, 'Barbara will never go home again; she swore she'd never go home because he, because Dad ... because Dad, you know, molested her.'"

I didn't say anything for a moment. "You mean, you knew all this time, before I wrote and told you?"

"I'll never forget it," Gladys said. "I called Barbara Gay, and we cried and cried and cried. We cried for a week. Here all along, we thought you kids at least were in a good home all those years—it wasn't much, but it was something. And then to find out that. To find out he had touched you like that.

"I mean, how can you tell? The social worker sent us pictures of you kids, and you looked fine. You looked happy. They looked like every other parent looked—how could we know?"

"Oh, Gladys," I said, "there wasn't any way you could tell. There wasn't any way."

"She wrote to us, and told us that you kids were fine, that you were in the choir and got straight A's in school ..."

"Wait, who wrote?"

"Why, Marie, your adoptive mother."

"But, but ... how did she write you?"

"Oh Barbara, you didn't know?"

"Know what?"

"Well, we found her through 'Confidential Chat.' My sister Grace called me up one day and was all excited, and I couldn't understand what on earth she was talking about. She kept saying, 'They must be your kids; they must be your kids. I know they are; I know they are.' Well, it turned out your mother—I hate using that word for her—had written a letter saying how lucky she was to have adopted you kids. And that whoever had them before her was wonderful because you kids were so well-behaved. And she signed it Mizpah."

"Yeah ... I know that—it means blessing. But I didn't know she wrote to you for all those years."

"She sure did. Anyway, what happened is, we called the *Boston Globe* and asked them for her name. But they wouldn't give it to us. But they said they'd send her a letter from us and maybe she would write back."

"So you sent her the letter and she wrote back."

"That's right. She sent pictures and everything."

"But she never told us kids that she was doing it."

"And I didn't know that—I thought you kids didn't want anything to do with me." She paused. "I thought that maybe you thought we didn't want you anymore."

"No. No. I never, I swear to you, I never thought that. I thought those fucking social workers didn't give a fuck about kids," I said. "Excuse my language. And why did Al and Marie adopt us anyway? We didn't need a home—we had a home. Why didn't they see that? If they cared about kids, they woulda seen that, and they would say, 'No, these kids have a home. Let's adopt some kids who need a home.' But they didn't give a damn about us."

"You know, Barbara, I think you're right. I remember something, and it seemed like nothing at the time, but looking back—you know, they came and visited you first and took you out for ice cream."

"Oh, yes. I remember that. They took us to a riverbank; I remember the river."

"Well, apparently, you three kids started arguing about a ball. You all wanted to play with it, and there was only one ball. So when they came back, they told me about it, and then Marie said, 'Well, they'll get used to it, because that's all they're going to have.' And at the time, it bothered me a little, but I forgot about it. But, why not get two more balls so you all would have balls to play with?"

"We never had any toys, Gladys. Bicycles once, but not toys." I stared off into space. "No new clothes either."

"It was funny, but when you kids were really small, right after they took you, all the pictures she sent of you kids, you were wearing the clothes I had given you when you were with us. Pretty clothes. We didn't have any money, but our neighbors up the street had three kids, two girls and a boy, just a little older than you were. And they dressed their kids beautiful. They gave us a lot of their clothes, and you kids looked so beautiful. Billy had the most handsome suits, and you girls had such pretty little dresses.

"I remember bringing you to church. We went to church every Sunday, and this other neighbor came up and said, 'My, don't those kids look wonderful.' And I looked at her, and I was so mad; it was like she expected you kids to have green heads or something because you were foster kids or something. I said, 'Well, what'd ya expect—they'd be ugly?' Oh, it just made me so mad. Because there was another woman who took in a foster child the same age as her own daughter, and she dressed that girl in rags. She didn't really care about her. But as far as we were concerned, you kids were our kids, our family, same as if you had been born to us. Oh, people are so ignorant."

We ordered the same meal at every other restaurant we ate at as well. And we talked and talked and talked. We couldn't get enough of each other.

Before she left, I felt I had to tell her about the day we were taken away.

"Gladys, that day, you know, the day we were taken away, I remember that, I remember sitting in the car with those strangers, and I remember watching you cry and Bill hold you. And I knew something terrible was happening, but I didn't know what it was."

"That was a terrible, terrible day. And those damn social workers! Bill had bought Susan a rocking chair, so she would have a place to watch television. She used to hang back, you know, and never get a seat because all you other kids took them all. So Bill bought her this rocking chair, and it was a fast and firm rule no one could sit in that chair except Susan. And oh, how she loved that chair.

"Well, the day the social workers came, Bill told them, 'Take this chair; you've got to take this chair.' The social worker, Frost, that was her name, said no. Bill insisted, and you know, I think he was so mad he wanted to hit her, and Bill wasn't like that. But she wouldn't take that rocking chair. She said you kids weren't to have anything that would let you know where you came from."

"Yes," I said, "that's how it was. You know what, Gladys? I remember that chair."

And so the circle closed again, but this was the final closure. I thought I had found my mother, Joan Audrey Morris Ohrstrom, and I had. I thought she was a hero or a victim, and she was neither and both. I thought my father was a hero and a villain, and he was neither. I thought DSS was staffed with insensitive, lazy, uncaring social workers, and it wasn't. I thought I'd never have a mother, and I was wrong. For if anyone was my mother, it was Gladys Power.

Gladys had rubbed my arms and legs every day when I didn't walk so that I would move again. Gladys didn't believe I was retarded, and through her care, I became a happy, healthy little girl. Gladys took all three of us children, ensuring we would stay together. She shared her family with us. She loved us in the mundane, daily ways in which parents, true parents, love their children. She fed us, she sheltered us, she loved us. She was affectionate, kind, encouraging, stern, structured, and ever present.

Through Gladys, I experienced the real love real mothers give. Through Gladys, I learned blame, resentment, and hatred are the ways of adults who refuse to grow up, and love, acceptance, and courage are the character of adults who struggle to understand themselves and their place in the world. Gladys gave me more than she can possibly comprehend; as far as I am concerned, she saved my life and saved my brother and sister from becoming insensate, cynical, cold monsters. She loved us and kept us together, so we could love, protect, and honor one another when the hell of child abuse fell upon our shoulders when we were too young to even know the term. Because of Gladys, Bill, Dana, Barbara Gay, and Patti, we knew love, and we knew how to love each other all through our childhoods.

If any other heroes exist in this tale, they are my sister, Sue, and my twin brother, Bill. Despite our fights and struggles, my sister, brother, and I protected one another as best we could whenever an outside foe, such as abusive parents, threatened us. When I was a child, the only issue that mattered to me was staying together with my twin brother and sister.

We didn't know or remember anything beyond a few bare scraps of our time with Gladys, but our loyalty and love, including the love she instilled in us, had become part of us.

I started this adoption search for a perfect family, for parents who would love me and protect me, but I had searched for a castle built of sand. The love that sustained me through my life was the love given so freely by Gladys and her family. The love I gave every day of my life was the love I felt for my twin brother and sister. By the time I was five, I already knew the most important lesson of life: all that matters is how well I honor the people I love, how much I let them love me, and how much I love them.

CPSIA information can be obtained at www.ICGtesting.com
Printed in the USA
BVOW03s1025181213

339424BV00009B/106/P